HYPEROBSCURE

A collection of 32 short stories to fill you with a sweet sensation of dread.

By Tor-Anders Ulven

HYPEROBSCURE
Copyright © 2020 by Tor-Anders Ulven

All rights reserved.
No part of this book may be used or reproduced in any manner, or transmitted in any form or by any means, electronic, mechanical, photocopying, recording or otherwise, without express written permission by the author.

This book is a work of fiction. Names, characters, businesses, organizations, places, events and incidents are either the product of the author's imagination or are used fictitiously. Any resemblance to actual persons, living or dead, events, or locales is entirely coincidental.

Cover design by Lou Ellen Allwood (@louceph)
Formatted by Michelle River

Digital ASIN: B087796MQR
Paperback ISBN: 9798638117207

DEDICATED TO MY LOVING WIFE AND SONS

Without you by my side, none of this would have been possible. Thank you from the bottom of my heart for always believing in me.

I would also like to thank all my friends, family, and fans. You guys rock, and as long as you dare visit my twisted universe, I will never stop writing.

CONTENTS

First Date. 9
The New Neighbor 13
It Comes From The Walls. 19
All Fun And Games 27
Can't Love a Dead Chick 31
A Life For a Life 39
I'm Here. 47
Mdłości. 51
The Fathomless Depths 67
The Nameless Street Ritual. 75
The Day I Fell Into The Sky 91
Something New Under The Sun 95
Blood On The Wall 101
The Pale Faceless Dancer. 115
Hank's Country Food Fair 123
Me, Mizell, And Inspector Hole-in-the-Face . . 127

My Friend Bug 151

Francine In The Dark 157

Patches 161

Dear Mom 171

Digging Up My Dad 179

The Day I Tried To Live 181

Mommy, Why Is My Face Inside-Out? 199

The Dinner Ritual 203

The Curious Case of Baby Jeanie 211

Six Deaths, Six Funerals, Six Lives 219

Living With The David Reyes Disorder 233

One-One-Eight 237

Monsters Don't Always Hide Under Your Bed . 245

The Pavlovian Piggy 251

Wiggle Your Toes 263

Sweet Daniel's Disturbing Drawings 267

ABOUT THE AUTHOR 275

FIRST DATE

I've never done anything like this before. Never sat down with a man opposite in this capacity. The anticipation is real and tangible. He keeps looking over at me, and I don't know how to react. Should I smile? Would a smile be too forward? Should I just look back, meet his gaze? Then what? Where does it go from there? Should I introduce myself? Maybe he is waiting for me to break the ice? Should I do something with my hands? They're just sitting here, limp and useless. My legs are aching, maybe I should shift my position. Would that be too weird? Do people do that? I really shouldn't, it might give off the wrong signal. Do I do anything with my eyebrows though? That's something I've definitely seen people do. Like raise one maybe? Or both? Oh no, he's still looking at me. I don't know what to do.

"Hello," he says.

Oh no, how do I respond do that? Can I reply with a simple 'Hello' back, or should I elaborate? Maybe I don't need to say anything? Maybe it would be enough to just smile, or wave my hand, or gesture somehow? I have to do something, I can't just sit here staring at him, that would just be too weird. A combination of a facial expression, bodily pose, and an alluring greeting would be perfect, but if I mess it up it could quite possibly have the opposite effect of that I want.

"Hi," I reply.

That didn't seem right at all. I can tell by the way the expression on his face changes that I screwed up somehow. That I misread the signals. Damnit, why do I always do this? Why can't I just be normal? Why can't I instinctively react to these social cues?

"Do you want something to drink?" he asks.

I was dreading this question. I am quite thirsty, but the information that could be extracted from the essence of the answer is theoretically limitless. Hot or cold? Lukewarm? Size? Shape? Color? Fizzled? People can't really fathom how much a single choice like this can reveal about a person. I want him to think I am interesting, sophisticated, mysterious, elegant. A person who has seen it all, yet still willing to explore, grow and evolve. Someone that can challenge and question, capable of both receiving and giving criticism.

"Water," I say.

Was that right? It's neutral, healthy even, but could it be defined as boring, dull, lacking in imagination? Did I just blow it? Was this it? I can't move, I'm physically unable to move. It's just too much to process, too much to read into. I desperately try to identify the expression on his face; it seems serious, yet intrigued. Cold, yet inquisitive. Maybe there's still hope?

"So," he says. "Let's talk about the bodies we found in your freezer."

THE NEW NEIGHBOR

Mr. Johnson always greeted me with a smile in the morning. He'd flaunt those pearly whites shamelessly, just barely noticeable under that crazy moustache (you know the one where it sort of looks like a crow has died trying to consume your nose), and he'd wave energetically as I walked down to my mailbox. I'd raise my hand idly and do the old "good morning neighbor"-routine, but I'd quickly retreat to avoid getting trapped in conversation. He was nice enough, but he was one of those extremely neat and extremely boring kind of people. If he caught you off guard you'd be talking about the weather for hours.

Mr. Johnson moved in next door a little over a month ago. The place had been empty for a year or so, ever since old man Gordon kicked the bucket. He didn't have many relatives, and it took them awhile to figure out who'd be taking over the property. After six months the deed was signed over to his nephew, who in turn tried to flip the place post-haste. But because of the nature of his uncle's death (he was found rotting in his basement a month after he died), there wasn't much interest.

Until Mr. Johnson came around.

He didn't seem to mind the history of the place at all. In fact, he'd brag about it constantly, as if the rot-stain on the concrete floor was some sort of trophy. It didn't bother me at first; I like a good cadaver-story just as much as the next guy, but when you factored in the moustache and that holier-than-thou smirk, it became increasingly tiresome.

And then I started noticing that he always seemed to have blood on his clothes.

I don't know when it started, but I know that after I first noticed it I couldn't not see it anymore. It was just so obvious, yet so indistinguishable. Everyday; clean clothes, fresh blood stain. On his sleeve, on the leg of his pants, on the collar of his shirt, on the tip of his boots. Just a little drop, a vague smudge of red, a little hint of the old crimson. And his smile was fading. Just a tad bleaker every morning. A little broodier, a little darker. Until it was gone.

I'd ask him about the blood sometimes. Just, you know, out of curiosity. You can't help it when you keep seeing it daily. You need answers. It's human nature.

"So," I'd say, "What's with the blood?"

"It's just paint," he'd say, avoiding eye-contact at all cost. "I've been redoing the basement."

And so it went. Every other day I'd ask again, and he would reply with some incompetent excuse that wouldn't hold up in court. I believed him for a bit, I'll admit it; he did seem like the type that would "redo" things just to have something to blab on about with his golf-buddies. But after the second week of "painting" my skepticism was skyrocketing. And with the accelerated decline of his smile, I knew something dubious was going on.

So one day I decided enough was enough, and just confronted him right there on the street.

"So," I said. "Wanna show me your basement?"

He stared at me for quite some time, his moustache dancing like a drunk caterpillar, his eyebrows raising and lowering like pinball flippers. I could see a drop of sweat forming on his forehead, slowly making its way down to the root of his nose. His eyes darted back and forth like they were following a phantom laser pointer.

"Sure," he eventually responded. "But, um, I'm not done redoing it yet, it's a bit messy."

I just shrugged. "I don't mind," I said. "I just want to see how it's coming along."

He nodded nervously and awkwardly ushered me up his driveway. I paced up to his door, and turned to face him. He seemed flustered, no doubt about it. He definitely had something to hide.

"In we go, then," he said weirdly as he opened the door.

I followed him in and looked around briefly as we walked towards the stairs leading to the basement. He'd really managed to fix the place up. Everything was sparkling new and shiny.

"Very nice," I noted. "You've been hard at work I see."

He nodded and gave me a half-hearted smile. "Yes, but the basement is proving to be quite a handful."

I followed him down the stairs into the basement. At first glance everything seemed perfect. Shiny hardwood floors covered the old concrete, the walls were painted in a tasteful crimson color, and he'd even replaced the old window with a stylishly profiled one. I raised my eyebrow inquisitively.

"This is spotless," I said. "I thought you said it was messy?"

He hanged his head in what I assumed to be shame. "Yes, but there's this thing," he pointed to the corner of the room. "Behind the sofa."

He walked over to the sofa and motioned for me to take a look. I followed close behind and peered over his shoulder.

"Ah, yes," I said knowingly. "I see what you mean."

"It keeps coming back," he complained. "I don't know what to do. It must be rust or something."

"I have an idea," I said staring into the back of his neck. "Forget all about it."

He turned to face me, his expression quite bewildered. I jabbed my knife into his jugular with some precision, and enjoyed the brief shower of blood before he sank down to the ground, a lovely pool of crimson steadily growing around him. It didn't take long before his heart gave up, and he just lay there motionless, his ridiculous moustache now slightly more tolerable tinted red.

"Is that still paint on your clothes?" I asked mockingly.

I hung his body head down from the ceiling with a rope I found in his garage. The last remaining pints of blood dripped into the bucket below, the soothing clunks and glops like chicken soup for the soul. I studied the stain hidden behind his sofa. It would appear I had a leak; the brown-red mush gathering in a stinking pond looking all too familiar. I suspected one of the pipes of my acid tanks needed some fixing. It must have seeped into the foundations, eventually ending up here. Such a shame really; it completely ruined the new hardwood floors.

When night falls I'll drag his body home and drop it into one of the tanks. It will take two days for the bones to dissolve. That should be enough time to fix the leak and clean up this mess.

I seriously hope the next owner doesn't have a moustache.

IT COMES FROM THE WALLS

I was eight when my brother Josh died. I remember it vividly even now. Every little detail from when we woke up, until his very last breath. He was two years older than me, and we would fight non-stop, like most siblings do. That day was no different. We got up early before our parents did, and raced down the stairs. He won, like he always did, and was able to claim what little was left in the box of cereal. I was so mad at him for that. After we had finished breakfast, we ran outside to play. It was a warm summer morning, and I can still imagine that wall of heat hitting me as I opened the front door. We played for hours without pause, and it remains one of the best memories I have of him.

He died around noon. A long drop, a crunch, and a snap. It all happened so fast. I just stood there frozen, watching as the pond of blood grew, and listening intently as his final, wheezing breath left his broken body. Shock, my parents said. I was in shock. They couldn't get me to speak for weeks. I observed when the ambulance arrived, the paramedics and the firemen running around shouting hysterically. Then the sirens dying out in the distance, my mom and dad left sobbing inconsolably. I stood silent as the funeral came. I held my breath as they lowered the coffin into the awaiting depths. And only after I saw the headstone loom before me could I allow myself to talk again.

We moved shortly after the funeral. My mom could no longer stand living in the house. My dad reluctantly agreed, but kept telling her that they would be losing money on the sale. Mom didn't care; no amount of money could have persuaded her to stay. To live on the property that stole her Josh from her. I knew then that nothing would ever be the same again.

The new house was quite a bit smaller than the old one; but I liked it. It was cozy and sweet, and had sort of an old cottage-vibe to it. And even though I missed Josh, I was happy to have a bedroom to call my own; to decorate as my own. To grow up in.

Days, weeks, and months passed, and not much changed. There was an aura of gloom about the family, a lingering grief that wouldn't quite let go. It was like the days just faded into nothing; like none of us really were there. Originally I thought that was the reason it came; it was drawn to our grief, to our constant ever-present sorrow.

The first time it came from the walls was three months after Josh's death. It was a day like all the others; grey and uneventful, and I had drifted off to sleep later than usual, my body maybe somehow aware that there was something unnatural nearby. I awoke in the darkness by an unidentifiable sound, somehow coming from all the walls at once. It was sort of a soft clicking sound, rising in pitch, then lowering again. I had never heard anything quite like it, and I sat up in bed squinting, trying to make out where it could originate from.

After a few minutes my eyes were slowly adjusting to the darkness, and my gaze was drawn to a hole in the wall. It was just a tiny knothole, maybe an inch or two, but for some reason I was convinced it was the source of the sound. I sat there for minutes trembling, just staring into the hole, not knowing why. Then I noticed it started widening, yet inexplicably remaining the same size. I crept under my sheets in fear when the head squeezed through. I just lay there, frozen, unable to move or make a sound. I could hear it moving around out there, like it was exploring, searching. I must have stayed under the sheets for hours before I finally just passed out.

The next morning I jolted awake with a scream, and immediately ran to tell my parents about it. They dismissed it of course; just some vivid dream caused by an overactive imagination they were sure. I tried to reason with them, but soon just gave up. They just wouldn't listen.

This kept happening for weeks. I would wake up to the soft clicking sound, stare at the hole, and hide under my sheets when I saw the head emerge. I could never get a good look at it; I was far too frightened, but it was completely bald and the skin had an ashen-grey complexion to it. I could never really judge the dimensions of it, because of the impossible nature of its arrival.

I would plead to my parent to just believe me, or let me sleep with them, or simply just explore the knothole, or tear down the walls, but they would dismiss me every time; usually just telling me I was being childish, that it was all just a nightmare, and that it eventually would stop.

One night I decided I wasn't going to hide anymore. I was going to face the thing that came from the walls. Figure out what it wanted. I was terrified, but resolute. I woke up like all the other nights, listening intently to that eerie clicking sound, staring at the knothole with absolute concentration. Swallowing deeply as the hole started to widen, and choking back my fear when the appalling head squeezed through. It landed on the ground with a thump, and I stared in horror as the tiny, underdeveloped body writhed on the floor, struggling with the weight of the oversized head. I let out a scream then. I just couldn't hold it in any more. The creature raised its head strainously, like an alerted animal, and stared directly at me.

There was holes. Nothing but holes. The mouth was a yawning chasm of nothing, the nose and eyes the same; just endless abyssal rifts. I screamed again, this time probably loud enough to wake up the entire neighborhood. My mom says she still has nightmares about that scream, and she'll easily admit it froze her blood to ice.

My parents came running into the room in a

hysterical frenzy, only to find me alone, curled up on the floor in a fetal position, screaming my lungs out. It took them hours to calm me down, and they said I only spoke nonsensical gibberish. They took me to my aunts for few days, but eventually I was forced to sleep in my own room again.

The ritual continued. I woke up, stared at the hole until the head emerged, then hid under my sheets for the remainder of my conscious night. I was slowly but surely getting used to it. I'd still tell my parents about it, but they still wouldn't believe me. I know it sounds horrible, but you have to understand they were still dealing with the death of Josh; they simply had no energy to indulge my self-induced traumas.

But at some point I got too used to it. I simply stopped waking up. The sound no longer bothered me, and I would just sleep through it. Problem solved, right? I certainly thought so.

Until I woke up one night with the thing on top of me, staring me right in the face. Those endless abyssal eyes swirling away, that gaping chasm of a mouth hovering inches above. I was too mortified to scream, my body now somehow unable to move at all. As an adult I could have simply written it off to some extreme form of sleep paralysis, if it wasn't for the next part.

Foul-smelling, black liquid started pouring from the creatures' orifices, completely covering, drowning, my face in it. My mouth was filling with the awfulness of it, and at some point I swallowed some, just to catch my breath. The taste was that of death. Of decay and rot. I was panicking, desperately trying to move, scream, do anything at all. But I couldn't. I was trapped. And sooner or later I just passed out.

I woke up in a pond of the black liquid.

I showed my parents the foul stuff, and explained what had happen. My dad said they had seen some signs of leakage around the house, so it must have been that. Just some stale, putrid water seeping through the roof. I resigned then. From ever asking them anything again. They simply couldn't be trusted.

We moved a couple of years later. I would see the creature every night, but made sure to set an alarm so that I never had to wake up to that horrible creatures' face ever again. But now I was free, I thought happily. We were getting along better as a family, and we were finally moving away from that cursed place. And for months I felt wonderful. I had a semblance of life again, of freedom, of joy.

But then, one night, I woke up to the soft sound of clicking. I sat up and scanned the walls. And there it was. A tiny knothole. And a head squeezing through it.

Moving didn't help at all. The creature followed me, wherever I went. I'd be free for a couple of months tops, then I would wake up to that sound. And that head. Every once in a while I would sleep through it, and wake up with that ashen-grey face inches from my own. The liquid would pour, and I would swallow. Then I'd wake up in a pond, with no one there to believe me.

I grew up depressed, stressed, unhinged, half-mad. Somehow I made it through school, college, even got a job. But it would never feel good. I could never feel joy. I could never connect with another human being ever again. The creature wouldn't let me. It slowly drained my life from me. When I was twenty-five my doctor told me my physiological age was that of a fifty year old. Start exercising, he said.

One day, three years ago, I went back to the place it all started. I had known for years already, maybe even always, what caused it, what brought it to me, what it was. But I could never take it in, never admit to it, never confess. And that was always the reason for my punishment.

I stood by the gaping chasm of the abandoned dried-up well where Josh had fallen in, staring into the depths.

I remember every moment of that day. Every detail vividly. I remember playing hide and seek. I remember hiding behind the garage. I remember seeing Josh looking for me around the well. He stood so close. So dangerously close. Then I remember how mad I was at him for eating the last of the cereal. And I remember creeping up behind him, and pushing him with all my might. Then an endlessly long drop, a loud crunch, a blood-curdling snap.

"I am sorry, Josh," I said then. "I didn't mean to do it. I thought it was just water."

But his vengeance is endless.

Endless like that drop.

Endless like the black of the creatures' eyes.

Endless like my suffering.
I will go to sleep tonight.
Every night.
Forever.
And it will come from the walls.

ALL FUN AND GAMES

A stone's throw away from our property there was a deep and dark and lovely forest. A place for adventures. Lydia and I would escape to this fantastical world whenever we could, usually to get away from our parents, who weren't very good people. We'd hide in the dense undergrowth when father came calling, but eventually he'd find us and punish us for disobeying him.

This day he was in a particularly bad mood. Lydia ran away first thing after school, with me in close pursuit. She was two years older than me, so I'd usually trail behind, but she would always stop and wait for me after a little while.

We played for hours. Our usual games, and a few new ones we'd come up with just to pass the slow hours until dusk.

"I can do way more than you," Lydia teased. "I'm older and stronger."

"Nuh-uh," I responded. "I can do a hundred, at least."

"No way," Lydia poked me in the shoulder. "And even so, I can do twice that, easy."

"Oh yeah," I said, "Well I can do a thousand."

"Two-thousand," Lydia quickly countered. "With my eyes closed."

"Ten-thousand," I poked her right back. "With one hand and my eyes closed."

This went on for a while. We were always competing, bickering, but in a friendly, sibling rivalry kind of way. Lydia would usually win. She was older and stronger after all.

We were too preoccupied with bragging and gloating and teasing to notice the movement in the bushes, the gentle rustling of the ferns, the lurking shadow in the distance.

"300,000," Lydia beamed. "No way you can beat that."

"Can too," I complained.

"Nuh-uh, " she said. "You're too small and weak Melinda."

She started tickling me, knowing full well that was my one great weakness. We laughed and rolled around in the tall grass, watching the sun slowly setting as we did. A dry twig snapped just down the hill, the sound reaching us just a little too late.

"So there you naughty girls are," our mother came rushing out of the bushes. "I sent your father out to find you hours ago. Where is he?"

Lydia shielded me behind her, like the perfect protective big sister she was.

"He's right here," Lydia smiled and pointed behind us. "He's been here a while."

"What do you mea-"

A horrifying scream echoed through the vast woods, the blood-curdling sound heard for miles. Our mother fell to her knees wailing, her face buried in her hands, her uncontrollable, pathetic sobs coming in erratic waves.

While I'm not sure we ever got to 300,000 stabs, one thing remains certain; there wasn't much left of his body for us to stab anymore. Lydia smiled at me and waved the knife teasingly.

"Wanna go again?" she asked. "I bet I can do it faster this time."

"Nuh-uh," I replied. "I'm gonna beat you this time."

We giggled and held hands as we approached our mother.

CAN'T LOVE A DEAD CHICK

I only knew Michelle for a month, but it was truly a month to remember. I first met her when she was carving out my high school bully's eye with a butter knife, and we were more or less inseparable after that.

She was a few years older than me, so of course I fell instantly in love, but I knew deep down we were destined for friendship and little else. I knew this deep down because she made it clear that she was gonna die in roughly a month. Can't love a dead chick, she'd say.

At first I thought it was just a clever way to avoid the awkwardness of turning me down, but at some point I came close to believing her. It was just something about her, something extremely...free. Careless and unconfined. Refreshingly brave and outspoken and honest.

When I met her I was going through the most depressing period of my life. I was constantly bullied and belittled at school, my younger twin sisters were both hospitalized, each needing a transplant to survive (Jenna needed a heart, Chloe needed kidneys), and my parents had their hands full covering the medical expenses. I think we all in our own ways were on the verge of just giving up, of just letting go.

I was saved by Michelle. I have no doubt about it. If she hadn't shown up when Brett was beating the shit out of me, I would have killed myself that day. I was just so sick of it, sick of the beating, sick of the abuse, sick of being alone. But Michelle came out of nowhere, threw him into the wall, knocked his nose half-way up his brain, and proceeded to dig out his left eye with the aforementioned cutlery. He never touched me again.

You'd think she'd get into to trouble after doing something like that. But it was never reported. Brett claimed it had been an accident, that he'd crashed with his moped. I think he feared that Michelle would kill him if he said otherwise. I for one have no doubt she would have. That was just who she was.

Michelle never went to school. She said it was because she knew she was gonna die. Why bother with bullshit like school then. No, she was all about enjoying life to the fullest, kicking assholes in the face, fucking over people who fucked over others. She wanted to leave this world a better place than she found it, and by her logic this was done exclusively by ridding it of shitbags, one way or another.

"How do you know you're gonna die?" I asked her once.

"My parents tell me," she said. "Every day. And they're good for their word."

She wouldn't explain it in detail. Just that she was raised knowing the exact date and time of her death, down to the very second. And that it was meant to be. That's what they told her. In death, her life would have meaning.

At first I didn't think much of it, you know. She was a crazy girl, and she always said weird stuff like that. I was kinda banking on it all being some bizarre joke or something, but when the month drew to a close, I was getting really worried it might all be true. I'd grown too attached to her. Every minute I wasn't at school or the hospital was spent with her, and the thought of losing her, my only friend, made me horribly depressed.

That last week I was really on edge. The twins were in bad shape, and my parents were spending every waking minute at the hospital. They had yet to find any donor matches, and time was running out. It felt like my time was running out too. The dark thoughts were returning, and I started imagining how I would kill myself should Michelle ever leave me.

I found it strange that she'd never invited me home. I mean, friends do that, right? Invite each other over. She'd been to our house several times, she even crashed on the couch a few times, and we would often watch movies there, raid my parents liquor-cabinet, get wasted and generally just have fun. But I'd never been to her house. Not once. I didn't even know where she lived.

So one night I just decided to follow her. What was there to lose, really? Maybe I could get some answers from her parents or something. Some way to explain why she was so convinced she was dying. Maybe they lied to her? Some sort of cult? A way to form her beliefs into accepting the unacceptable. A way to control her.

I stalked her for thirty minutes, lurking in the shadows as she paced down the streets. When she headed to the outskirts I started getting worried, and when she took the narrow trail through the forest I was almost having a full on panic-attack. Where the hell was she heading? As far as I knew, there weren't any houses for miles.

About halfway into the forest, I suddenly lost her. It was like she vanished without a trace. I walked back and forth, up and down, but there was just no sign of her at all. Eventually I had to give up and return home, my mind growing ever darker.

I remember the last day like it was yesterday. Every minute of it, crisp and clear and vivid in my mind. Every scent, every sound, every muscle moving on her perfect face, all those smiles and kind words. Everything.

The last day came and went, but I didn't know it was the last day. If I'd known, I would have told her how much I cared for her, how much she meant to me, how much I owed her my life and sanity. Without her I wouldn't be alive. But I didn't know, and I never told her. I hope she somehow realised it, that she could see it in my eyes and actions every day, but I can never be sure.

She just acted so normal, you know. She was

Michelle that day too. Same carefree spirit, the same wild, devil-may-care attitude. We spent the afternoon smoking weed, watching silly cartoons, laughing and just enjoying each others company.

But when she left, I knew something was up. I don't know how. I guess there was some detail, some little thing that alarmed me, but having replayed and analyzed that day over and over in my mind, I can't think of anything. Nothing. But I knew.

So I followed her again. This time I stayed closer, always having her in my sights, always knowing exactly where she was. She was walking considerably slower that night, almost like she knew I was behind her. Almost like she wanted me to follow her. The air was cold and crisp, and whenever autumn draws close, I can step outside, take a deep breath, and relive the exact moment when she suddenly turned on her heels to face me.

"This is it," she said. "This is the day I die."

She walked over to me and handed me an envelope. It was light, but there was definitely something in it. A letter perhaps.

"You will need this," she stroked my hair gently. "When the time comes, you'll know what to do with it."

"I don't understand," I said. "Please, let's just leave. Let's just get out of here."

She smiled and kissed me on the cheek. If I concentrate real hard I can still conjure up the smell of her perfume.

"This is goodbye," she murmured softly. "But you will come to understand that it was always meant to be."

I reached out to hug her when they emerged from the darkness. Two tall figures clad in dark robes, an old man and an elderly woman, their milky-white hair flowing gently in the breeze. They had this solemn expression on their faces, the kind you'd see in funerals, an expression of acceptance to sorrow and despair because it is just a part of life. Michelle pushed me away forcefully, and by the time I'd regained my balance it was already too late.

Her throat had been slit from either side of her neck. A perfect cross, left to right, right to left. Blood was squirting out, coloring the dull brown of the roadside a deep shade of crimson. The robed couple swiftly stepped back into the shadows, leaving me desperately clutching the lifeless body of Michelle, screaming my lungs out, wailing like an animal into the cold night.

The paramedics came ten minutes later. I have no idea who called them. Anonymous, they later told me. She had no ID on her, so they asked me a bunch of questions. I didn't know the answer to any of them. She was Michelle. That was all I knew. Her name was Michelle. She was my friend, and she was the best person I'd ever met.

They let me ride the ambulance to the hospital, but they quickly pronounced her dead. She'd lost too much blood, they told me. It wasn't my fault. There wasn't anything I could have done. This didn't offer me much comfort. I was devastated. Totally broken, the dark thoughts resurfacing once again, this time with more power than ever before.

"What's that in your hand," one of the paramedics asked. "Does that belong to Michelle?"

I glanced at the envelope. It was completely drenched in blood, much like me. And then it suddenly hit me. I don't know what it was, but it was like she told me; when the time comes, you'll know what to do with it. So without thinking, I just handed it over to him. He sort of held it up, like he'd somehow see through it if he got a better angle of it, before he gently opened it.

"Well, I'll be damned," he said.

I am better now. I still have problems understanding what happened, but I am better. I have come to terms with it. With the fact that everything happened just the way it was supposed to happen. And it has shaped me, shaped my life into what I am today. Michelle didn't just save me. She saved my entire family. Every aspect of my life.

And I guess you're wondering what was in that envelope. Maybe you'd figured it out, maybe not.

It was a donor card. And as it turned out, she was a perfect match for my twin sisters.

Can't love a dead chick, she said.

That's the only thing she was ever wrong about.

A LIFE FOR A LIFE

I'm not crazy. I'm not fucking insane. This I know. This is a fact. I haven't been hallucinating, haven't been tripping on acid, there's no fucking tumour growing in my brain, I don't have any history of mental illness at all. So I did not make this up. This happened. This is real. Remember that.

I can't say exactly what made me wake up, if it was the metallic scent in the air, or if it was the warm, sticky feeling of the blood slowly pooling in our bed, but I remember screaming bloody murder once I realised what was going on. My wife, Darla, hardly registered the noise, she just sort of snorted groggily, eyes all dull and glassy.

"What's going on?" she mumbled.

"You're bleeding!" I yelled, "Oh my god, oh my god, oh my god."

I panicked. I could tell by her condition that it was serious. She'd lost a lot of blood, and she looked pale and unfocused. All I could think of was the worst case scenarios. Death, still birth, both of the above. Her gaze was far away, like she had problems staying conscious, and I finally snapped into action, lifted her up, and ran frantically to the car.

The drive to the hospital was hazardous to say the least. I swerved into oncoming traffic several times, breaking more or less every existing traffic law, barely even focusing on the road for most of the drive. It's a wonder I didn't kill us all. But I couldn't stop myself. I couldn't imagine my life without her. That's all I could think about. Get to the hospital. Get to the hospital before it's too late. Please God, don't let her die.

I didn't bother parking the car. I drove it right up to the entrance, left it running in neutral, grabbed Darla, ran inside yelling hysterically for someone to come help me. Help her. I honestly can't remember much of what happened next. Someone came along and took her from me, put her down on a bed, rushed away in a hurry. Next thing I know I'm just standing there, covered in blood, answering all sorts of questions.

"She's eight months pregnant!" I sobbed, "Please, just save her. Please, please, please."

"Calm down, sir," some faceless nurse said, "We're gonna do everything in our power to save your wife. But you have to calm down. You need to help us help her."

I couldn't calm down. I don't think it's humanly possible. Not when someone you love is in danger. When someone you love is about to die. Not when you can't do anything about it. All you have to grab onto is worry, distress, panic, fear, sorrow, sadness, and that's the only thing that keeps you sane. I stood there shivering, convulsing, tears flowing, gasping for air, trying to the best of my ability to answer the questions. To help them save her.

"Thank you, sir," the faceless nurse said, "Please, sit down. I'll get back to you as soon as we have some news."

Sit down? Sit down?! All I wanted was to scream, lash out, hit something, make the pain on the inside manifest on the outside instead, and they wanted me to sit down? I knew it wasn't their fault. I knew I had no choice. But still it felt so...pointless. I hate not being in control. Hate feeling useless. Hate having to wait for someone else to fix it.

I slouched down and buried my face in my hands. I couldn't believe this was happening. Not to us. Not now. My mind was racing, and it was always the most ridiculous, insignificant notions I got hung up on. Like how I was gonna miss work. I had a major presentation in a couple of days. Important stuff. Or how disappointed my parents would be if I didn't become a dad. Or how I dreaded calling Darla's parents to tell them the bad news.

"Don't you just love this place," a cheery voice suddenly said.

I raised my head to identify the owner of the voice. I could have sworn I was the only one around, and I couldn't recall hearing anyone else walking in. But there he was, sitting right next to me. He was young, maybe in his mid-twenties, long blonde hair, dressed in jeans and a white hoodie. He smiled happily as my tear-filled, bloody visage greeted him with shock and disbelief. He had perfect teeth. I remember this vividly. Perfect.

"What the fuck do you mean?" I spat angrily.

I wasn't really myself, and having some douchebag fucking with me when my wife's life was hanging in the balance? I wasn't having it.

"Hospitals, man," he chuckled, "The lovely scent of misery and death. So invigorating."

I immediately saw red. I wanted to take a swing at him so badly, but something inside me held me back. I can't explain it, but it was like I knew it would be a horrible idea.

"Shut the fuck up," I shouted, "My wife's in there. She's fucking dying for all I know."

He threw his head back and laughed heartily.

"She sure is," he smiled, "Sweet, sweet Darla. Far too young to bleed out in a hospital bed, don't you think?"

I stared at him with wide-eyed shock and anger. How the fuck did he know? Was he here when I brought her in? Why hadn't I noticed him before now then?

"Wh-what?" was all I could muster, "How the fuck…"

He chuckled, "I know everything, Nick. I know that right now Darla's dying. She's losing too much blood. They can't stop it."

He smiled and leaned in close. His eyes sparkled a hypnotizing emerald green, but I couldn't focus on anything but the smell. It was a lovely fragrance, sweet flowers and fruits. My wife's fragrance.

"I give her five minutes," he grinned, "Then the doctors will come through that door, and your life will never be whole again."

"But the…" I started, tears filling my eyes again. I couldn't help but to believe him. Every fiber of his being radiated truth and sincerity.

"Ah, the life inside her?" he pointed to his stomach, "They'll save it. You'll be a single parent, grieving widower, destined for a life of hardship and perpetual disappointment. You'll drink yourself to death eventually. No one will miss you. C'est la vie."

I tore at my hair in despair. His words slithered into my mind, lingering, echoing in there, their hollow, somber meaning burrowing into my consciousness, imprinting on it a hopeless, dreary, unforgiving existence.

"N-No," I sobbed, "Th-There has to be something, some way…"

He tapped his nose and grinned widely, "Funny you should say that…"

"Wh-what do you mean?" I said, "What the fuck do you mean?!"

He smiled and stood up from his seat. He was tall and slim, but at the same time he appeared unnaturally imposing, like he was emanating pure unfiltered strength. It felt like I was cowering beneath him, like I was nothing but an insignificant ant he could stomp out of existence should he so will it.

"A life for a life," he reached out his right arm, "Your wife's life, to be exact."

I just stared at the hand. What the fuck did he mean, a life for a life? What the fuck was going on here? Who the fuck was this guy?

"It's real simple, Nick," he bent down and whispered to me, "I'll save your wife, but in return you'll have to let me take another life."

I was still staring at the hand, my body tense and rigid. It felt wrong on so many levels. Unnatural, unholy, something that should never transgress.

"Who?" I asked, "Who will you take instead?"

He grinned, "That's always the question, isn't it? It's not life itself that's precious; it's the life you're familiar with."

"Who?!" I demanded.

"Don't worry, Nick my boy," he chuckled, "It won't be someone you know. A perfect stranger, someone you've never even met. And it will be like they never existed. Gone. Vanished. No trace of them. It's a once-in-a-lifetime deal, Nicky. I'd take it if I were you."

I shivered uncontrollably. There were dark forces at work here, that much I knew. Blasphemous powers. But I didn't hesitate. I didn't even consider it. How could I? It was my wife, my one true love. I stood up and shook his hand.

"Attaboy, Nicky," he laughed, "You won't regret this. You might even thank me one day."

"One da-" I started, but was interrupted by a

doctor rushing through the door from the E.R. When I turned back to face the man, he was gone. Vanished. What was weirder still, was that it still felt like I was holding his hand, like we were still locked in that grim handshake.

"Mr. Matthews," the doctor took my hand, "Good news. Your wife is doing well. She's weak and exhausted, but doing excellent considering the circumstances."

I laughed. And cried. A wholesome, wonderful combination of the two. She was alive. She was well. I'd never been happier in my entire life. But then a thought occurred to me. A dark thought.

"And the…" I muttered, "I mean, the…"

"Oh, you mean the baby?" the doctor smiled, "Don't worry, your son is in perfect health. We had to do an emergency C-section, but he's a strong one. You can see them both soon."

"Son…" I whispered, "A son…"

I'm not crazy. I'm not insane. This is real. I told you to remember that.

They were fine. Fine and happy and healthy. The two of them. Mother and son. But I couldn't enjoy it. Couldn't believe it. My wife didn't understand. Why wasn't I happy? Why was I acting so strange?

I haven't been hallucinating. I haven't been tripping on acid. I went with my wife to every doctor's appointment, every ultrasound, every physical checkup. I was there every step of the way.

There's no tumour growing in my brain. No fucking history of mental illness.

So why do they look at me like I'm mad? Why can't they just believe me? I did not make this up. This happened. This is real.

I remember everything so vividly. But now it's gone. Vanished. No trace. Like it never existed in the first place.

I remember my wife being pregnant.

Pregnant with twins.

I'M HERE

"He can't hear you, miss."

Yes, I can.

"Are you sure?"

I'm right here.

"Quite. Henry is in a coma, I'm afraid. Not much we can do for him right now."

Nonononono, I'm right here.

I recognize the voices. My girlfriend, Ada, and... someone else. Deep male voice. A doctor? Doctor Kaczynski? Why can't I open my eyes? Why can't I move my legs? My arms?

Why is Ada crying?

"He suffered major head trauma in the crash, miss. Even when the swelling goes down, I'm not sure he'll ever come out of it."

Ah, yes. Car crash. I remember now. I was driving...home? From visiting Ada's parents. Nice people. Her father seemed to take quite a shine to me. I was like the son he never had, he told me. Very cliché I suppose, but sort of sweet. We had chicken for dinner. Delicious.

"When, uh, when do you know more?"

Then, a long stretch of road, up by Fletchers Peak I think, old man Johnson's farm. I was stuck behind a car, a van, one of those animal transports. Horses maybe? Cattle?

"A few days, miss, maybe more. But like I said, I wouldn't get my hopes up."

I'm here, Ada. Don't listen to him.

Who was that driving? Why did I swerve off the road? The car in front of me hit a pothole or something, there's quite a few of them up there you know. The back door of the van swung open.

"Oh, uh, I'll be back tomorrow then."

Nononono, Ada, come back. I'm here. I can hear you!

The back door of the van swung open. Something rolled out. I remember hitting the brakes hard. No real thought behind it. Pure instinct. The car stopped inches away from it. From her. But she wasn't alive, was she? All mashed up to minced meat. But the others were. Alive, I mean. I could see them squirming back there. Three of them, all chained together in the back of that van. Naked and bloody and whimpering and hurting.

"I'm glad we got that sorted, Henry."

Come back Ada. I'm still here.

I remember the driver. Don't I? Familiar face. Familiar voice.

"I'm sorry, Henry, but I can't have you talking about what you saw."

Shit, nononono, wait, wait, wait.

"I still can't believe you survived that, Henry. I was so sure I took care of you."

Fists and elbows to the face, Doctor Kaczynski dragging me out of the car. He must've beaten me into an unrecognizable pulp. When I came to again, my car was rolling down the hill. Nothing I could do. Watch as the rocks got bigger. Hear the screeching symphony of the car crumpling. Feel the steel carapace wrap itself around my body. Succumb to the darkness embracing me.

"Don't worry, I won't fail again. It's time for another nap, Henry, and I'm quite certain this one will be permanent."

No.

Not yet.

I'm here, Ada.

I'm here.

MDŁOŚCI

The train ride was two hours. Two hours spent in dim, flickering light, watching a fat old lady eat what I'm convinced was rancid cat food from a dirty plastic bag. Not pellets, mind you. No, it was the sludgy, oozing, disgusting stuff; bits of liver and entrails and eyes and fat, all mashed together into something vaguely edible. She dug her fingers into it shamelessly, licking them clean in a sickening display of social ineptitude, all the while looking me dead in the eye. I could have looked away. But some things, hideous as they may be, simply has to be observed in order to be believed.

Zeke was waiting for me at the end of the line. Some godforsaken outpost in the middle of nowhere. I could say that I don't even remember the name, and it wouldn't be a lie per se; it's just that it doesn't seem important anymore.

"Tommy!" Zeke yelled excitedly as I got off the train. "T-Dawg!"

I raised my hand in greeting, but secretly wanted to punch his face in. We had a falling out a couple of years back, and we really hadn't been talking since.

There was a woman. There's always a woman. Except Zeke ran off with this particular one. Left me high and dry and heartbroken. Rumour has it that it all ended in a spectacularly messy breakup, culminating in her glorious destruction of his precious vinyl collection. Karma I suppose you'd call it. I always wondered what happened to her.

"Zeke," I said. "Good to see you man."

I lied of course. If I had any other choice, I'd fucking ignore his hysterical phone call. But I needed the money. And he did sound sincere. But still, I should have known better. Should have read the signs. Should have spotted the red flags.

"Likewise man, likewise." He gave me an awkward hug. I could see it already then, in his tired gaze. Red-veined eyes. Dilated pupils. He was on something. And a lot of it. But I didn't care. I was there for the money. In and out, one night. That was the deal.

"So," I said. "What am I doing here exactly?"

We walked to the parking lot, about five minutes from the station. Zeke had already smoked three cigarettes before we reached his car. I could see his hands shaking uncontrollably. Was it the drugs? Alcohol? Or something else entirely?

"I'm in some real deep shit here, Tommy," he said. "But I think I found a way out."

He was a pale, sweating, shivering mess, barely able to stay on his feet most of the time. Zeke had always been long and thin - gaunt I guess the word is - but not like this. There was hardly anything but skin and bones, and his sickly appearance, namely the hollow-cheeked face and sunken eyes, made me feel increasingly uncomfortable.

I snatched the car keys from his fingers. "I think I'll drive," I said. "You don't look so good." He nodded weakly, and staggered to the passengers side.

"Just need you to watch my back tonight," he mumbled. "You know karate and shit, right?"

"What? No," I stared at him quizzically. "I went to Judo for like a month when I was eleven. Haven't been in a fight since pre-school."

"But you won though, right?" he tried to smile. "Look, I don't expect anything to happen, but you're a big guy, and I just need you to stay close. Just in case."

I nodded thoughtfully and started the car. "So where to?" I asked. He'd mentioned something about a party, so I figured it would be close to, I guess you'd call it a town?, maybe a bar, or a club, or something.

"See that road," he pointed ahead. "Follow that north for about an hour and we should be getting close."

If you didn't know Zeke you'd probably think it was a joke. But I knew Zeke, and I didn't. He had this skill - some might go as far as to call it a superpower - where he'd find a party wherever he was, or, failing that, make a party happen wherever he was. So when he told me we were going to an abandoned house in the middle of goddamn nowhere I didn't even give it a second thought; that was just how Zeke rolled.

"Hey man," he said a few minutes in. "About that

whole Lydia business…"

"Don't," I glanced at him. He was more or less unconscious, his head dangling from side to side, the weight of it suspended only by the seat belt, of which I forced him to put on.

"It's the past," I continued. "Besides, I hear she wasn't much of a keeper anyway."

He laughed then. A horrible, raspy, discordant sound, his body convulsing and spasming, like it wouldn't allow him even the slightest glimmer of joy. I suddenly felt nauseous, but I can't begin to explain why. Maybe, for the briefest of moments, I knew what was coming. Knew what awaited me in that godforsaken house.

Zeke kept slipping in and out of consciousness for most of the drive, but the moment we approached the side road leading to the house he suddenly jolted awake, his eyes wide with what I then could only assume was anticipation. The promise of booze, drugs and women, not necessarily in that order, would do that to him. Whatever state he was in, no matter how fucked up he'd be; mention any one of the above, and watch him come back to life like some freaky mechanical automaton.

"That's it," he said. "That's the place."

I felt sick to my stomach. Framed against the vicious blood red sky, the house was bleakly grey and harrowing, casting unnaturally ominous shadows down the rough, overgrown driveway. It looked ancient, century-old or more, and I couldn't even begin to imagine what kind of parties went on in that creepy shithole. There were a couple of cars parked out front. But I heard no music. And I saw no lights.

"You sure?" I said hesitantly. "This death-trap?"

"Don't judge a book by the rotting wooden carapace surrounding it," he said poetically.

I parked the car haphazardly on what could have once been the front lawn, but now resembled a wildly spreading weed forest, and got out. Zeke followed, his lanky, trembling frame lurching unsteadily towards the front door. I don't know, but to me it almost seemed like he was deteriorating by the minute. Rapidly rotting away, just like the ramshackle eye-sore we were approaching.

"Look, man, about Lydia," he murmured. "I really am sorry, you know."

"Hey, forget it, " I said. "I've moved on. We're good."

Were we good though? I guess his current physical and mental state somewhat dulled whatever resentment I still held for him. Right now I just wanted to get him out of that house alive; I could always punch him in the face later.

"Let me do the talking, alright?" he said. "These guys don't fuck around."

"Jesus Z, what the fuck have you dragged me into?"

Zeke didn't reply, just gave me a sad, terrified look as he opened the door. I felt a rush of adrenaline enter my system, guided undoubtedly by fear, as I realised how little I knew about our current situation. I had no idea what I was getting into. Who were these people? What did they want with him? I'd been too focused on the money and Zeke to even begin to question the nature of our visit to this desolate hellhole.

"Come on," he said. "Let's get this over with."

I followed him quietly inside, sensing as I crossed the threshold a significant change of ambience, like a sudden barometric pressure drop.

It's like...some places are just different, you know? Or, not even the places, more like...an intangible, contagious perception of the things that happened in those places. Could happen in those places. My best example would be the feeling you get when you wander the empty hallways of a hospital at night. Pale lights, off-white walls, deafeningly silent soundscape, lingering scent of the unknown. Maybe it's the smell of life? Maybe it's the smell of sickness? Maybe it's the smell of the dying?

I almost turned around right then and there, overcome by a flood of bad memories and painful mistakes, but Zeke quickly snapped me out of it. It was like he knew; knew what crossing that threshold would conjure up inside me.

"Hey!" he grabbed my arm. "Come on!"

The inside of the house was somehow even more dreary than the exterior. There was no color anywhere; faded, rotting, grey wood and decaying furniture, devoid now of any functionality whatsoever, swirling dust, an eerie beam of pale light penetrating the torn curtains, illuminating briefly the current inhabitants of the place. At first I didn't notice them. They blended in almost perfectly, like living black-and-white photos amidst the formless, ageless rubble.

"You just hang back, yeah?" Zeke whispered. I nodded weakly, the sight of them slowly registering, creeping from eyes to brain to stomach, lingering then as a sensation of loathing and sickness. But why? By all accounts they were utterly unremarkable. Not at all what I was expecting.

There were three of them. Centered on the floor of what I'm assuming was the living room (but there was only one room?) sat an old, wrinkly, bald man, maybe in his late eighties, dressed in an old-timey tweed suit, you know the type; the ones that always seem three sizes too large and only come in depressing shades of green-brown.

Behind him, barely noticeable at first, was a young woman. She was short, yet somehow incredibly imposing, like her very presence unconsciously demanded attention. She wore, you know, normal clothes, I suppose. It's the kind of stuff you can't really remember. Maybe black pants? White top? I can only ever imagine her face clearly, the rest sort of fades into blurry maybe's and I guess'es. But her face, and those huge, unblinking pale-blue eyes, I don't think I'll ever forget.

The boy sat at her feet. I don't believe he ever looked directly at me. Just sat there staring at the floor, fingers idly tracing the edge of the planks hidden under a thick layer of dust. He immediately struck me as strange. Well, stranger. I don't know, but there was just something about him that didn't feel right. Maybe it was the weird outfit; he was dressed like an old fashioned paperboy, you know, with the newsboy cap and short pants with suspenders and everything. Or maybe it was the fact that he never seemed to stop frowning.

Zeke sat down on the floor opposite the old man. What followed next remains unclear. It's not that I don't remember it; it's more that I remember several versions of it, and - to me at the very least - they're all equally true, and at the same time they're all equally false.

This would keep happening. Memories duplicating, changing ever so slightly, sometimes layered on top of eachother, to a point where it would be nigh impossible to separate one from the other. Was it his right hand or left hand? Who gave him the knife? Was there even a knife? There had to be, right? If not, where did all the blood come from?

I remember whispering. Or was it shouting? Zeke whispering to the old man, the old man shouting to Zeke. Possibly the other way around. Possibly neither, sometimes both. Sometimes simultaneously. Like a synchronized mantra. Pre-rehearsed, even? There didn't seem to be any words, at least not any I could easily decipher from the low, buzzing hum, or alternatively the discordant thunderous booms, of their vocal chords. Just aggressive hissing, violent murmurs, a swarming cacophony of shouting and/or whispering, all inexplicably attacking my ears from nowhere and everywhere at once.

Then, for a brief moment, clarity and silence, as the young woman silently approached me. Her face was pale as a freezing winter night, black as the eclipsed sun, impossible shades and colors, but also nothing more than a woman. Cheekbones to die for, sometimes to kill for, eyes bigger than her face, but still perfectly aligned on either side of her nose, vertically, probably horizontally too. Her lips were like twin dancing cobras, although not at all, yet that's how I remember them.

"Wanna get high?" she asked.

Sometimes she had a foreign accent. Sometimes not. Sometimes she didn't even talk. She looked up at me, and I realised suddenly that I was almost twice her size, yet I found myself cowering in her harrowing shadow.

"I'm Irina," she said, although sometimes she'd say Elena instead. Nadya too. They're all true I believe, but also false.

I didn't answer. Just looked nervously over at Zeke. He gave me a nod and a smile, enforcing his chosen stance with a trembling thumbs up, before turning back to the old man and continuing whatever it was they were doing. For the next few minutes Zeke would shoot me brief, worried glances, but even if I'd somehow understood what was going on, it'd already be too late.

Irina held a black pill, sometimes a capsule,

between her right (sometimes left) thumb and index finger, and was slowly guiding it towards my mouth. She was too short though, or I was too tall, one or the other, so I had to awkwardly bend down to accept the gift. She smiled, licked her lips, a darkness erupting from the impossible depths of her eyes.

"What is it?" I asked.

"Mdłości," she whispered into my ear as I swallowed the pill (sometimes capsule).

"I like the sound of that," I said.

The room started spinning. I say room, but I guess it was the house; there were no walls dividing anywhere from everywhere else. The boy was suddenly standing. He still didn't look at me, but his face was turned in my direction now, eyes slowly going white as the pupils disappeared up into his forehead. Irina was holding my hand and laughing, twirling in perfect harmony with the sudden amorphous nature of the house. I could be hallucinating at this point. It is entirely plausible. But then again, there's always the wretched possibility that I wasn't.

Then came the incident with the knife. Was it a knife? Sometimes it was there, other times it was just the blood. But there were no screams, no chaos, no disorder, or anger, or fear. That scared me even more than watching Zeke gut the old man, with or without the knife. The look on Zeke's face. The look on the old man's face. Irina's hysterical laughter. The white-eyed frowning boy. There was no response to it. Like it just casually happened.

"I'm sorry about Lydia," Zeke said. "I really am."

But I didn't believe him. That's the only thing I could think about as I fell to the floor, my body suddenly utterly unresponsive and limp. He was never sorry about Lydia. He was sorry about me.

"I'm really sorry."

Things slowly faded to black, like a beautiful coffin-lid sliding perfectly in place over my eyes, and I found myself smiling. Or was that someone else? Regardless, I can't really call it a dream, or sleep, or unconsciousness; it was more like a hazy fast-forwarded version of events I couldn't control. I think, I believe, I was somewhat conscious every step of the way, but I have no way of knowing for certain. How much time had passed? An hour? Two? A day? No way to tell.

I could move again in the darkness. Slowly, painfully at first. It took minutes, hours, before I finally regained enough mobility to stumble to my feet. I spent that time face down on the floor, focusing on my strained erratic breathing, listening to the frantic drumbeat of my heart. I was somewhere else, that much I realised. Concrete floor, stone walls, abyssal darkness.

Perpetual nausea.

It was like my intestines were boiling; but not with pain directly, more like they were filling with a tepid, lukewarm, acidic liquid, the foaming foulness climbing ever higher up my throat. No matter how hard I tried, there was no ignoring it; it remained a physical presence, a constant, relentless sickness, fused now with my very being.

Then came the smell. A rank odour I couldn't identify, but somehow instinctively knew by heart. Or is it knew by nose? I suppose it's a primal thing, encoded in our DNA, remnants from a time when it was necessary, essential even, to recognize the stench of death. It served as a warning I'd imagine. Where there is death, there are threats. Quite simple, really.

At first I didn't know what to do with it. I was hanging onto the possibility that the gut-wrenching nausea had something to do with the smell, so I tried breathing exclusively through my mouth, crawled up in a corner, anxiously trying to piece together exactly what had happened to me.

And then it began.

Violent spasms, brutal convulsions, my stomach twisting inside and outside of itself, exploding muscles pushing it up and through my ribs; a crack then - something snapping - but the pain hardly even registering; focus remaining solely on the oozing, chunky liquid lumpy, mass, nugget, presence - pressing ever upwards - esophagus stretching impossibly, expanding and pulsating and writhing; the nausea, sickness, vomit now too physical, too tangible, spewing forth from the mouth, nostrils, eyes; but it wasn't liquid, was it?, yes - but also no - an interconnected pool of black slimy puke, maybe soft bones, mucus bones, elastic upchuck; squirming and wriggling and slithering in a pool of itself, misshapen, malformed - not yet formed? - a birthing through the mouth then, but of what I wondered; abomination, abhorration, repugnance, detestation - Mdłości.

And then it ended.

As fast as a written sentence it was over, but your mind conjures a book before you even get that first word down, and the madness felt all too much like an eternity as I disgorged my unspeakable baby into existence. I couldn't move; every muscle and bone in my body now strained and worn and broken, my sanity gently floating in that comforting void of nothingness and everythingness combined, a place where the impossible suddenly loses its prefix, and you find yourself dying to die or disappear or shrink into the cracks of the floor.

I was brought back from that place by my black vomit-baby's first screams. My face was buried in it, and it was hurting, desperately trying to break free from the constraints of the birth canal. It had features now; feet, legs, torso, arms, hands, face, but they were all either angled wrong or placed wrong or had too many wrongs. I could barely keep my eyes open, barely stay conscious, and I could have just closed them, could have just passed out or on, but some things, disgusting as they may be, simply have to be observed in order to be believed.

It moved with the grace of all things ungraceful, like a spider without legs, or a slug with hooves, or a worm with one wing, the mucusy bones squishing against the floor as it feverishly tried to crawl away from me. But it couldn't. It was still stuck in my throat, and my nose, and my eyes. It kept screaming in horrible, high-pitched sonic outbursts, like how I imagine stomping down on a million fat maggots would sound like; air and gooey innards forcibly pushed out through every cavity, existing or not, in the blink of an eye (in fact I've tried it since, and it comes pretty close).

At long last it ripped itself free, the last remnant of it's puke-body slowly pouring from me, and within moments it was gone. Swooped up into the awaiting embrace of the old man. Where did he come from?, someone thought, probably me. Also, wasn't he dead? My eyes couldn't move that far from my face, so I never got a good look at him, but he was alive, how else could he be there?

"Well done, my friend," he said.

And then he ate my unholy vomit-baby. Consumed it, limb for limb, feasting, drooling, the liquid flesh dripping down in pulpy chunks onto the floor before me. It screamed every second of the ungodly act, the high pitched, maggot-stomping wails echoing in that room for minutes after. If I wasn't sick before - and I was - I was truly feeling it now. But not a physical ailment this time around. A sickness of the soul. A taint on the spirit. The extinguishing of every human aspect of my being.

"We leave you now," the old man said. "But you are strong. Just like your friend."

I tried to move my mouth, form words, communicate, when I saw him. Zeke. He was behind the old man, barely conscious, his haggard presence swaying unsteadily next to Irina and the frowning boy.

"The next one will be mine, yeah?" Zeke murmured. "That was the deal."

"You have served us well," the old man said. "And you will be rewarded."

Zeke didn't look at me once. Just kept staring at the floor. Soon after, when they disappeared, he followed hesitantly. But just as he reached the doorway, lips quivering, tears in his eyes, he turned to me.

"I'm sorry about Lydia," he said. Then he left.

And just like that I was alone in the darkness again. To be quite honest, I slightly favor the darkness nowadays. But did I then? The unseen, the unseeable? I find it comforting to know that there are things I cannot perceive, cannot observe, cannot ever know. But I ramble, I do that a lot these days; digress and keep going, not quite knowing where and what and who to end it all on. Zeke? Haven't seen him since that day. The old man? Sometimes I think I see him. I know I don't want to, but I don't think it works that way.

The door was open. I must have been there for days - it sure felt like it - but I was able to crawl out of that room, soon realising I was still in that house, in the cellar of it, crawling then, inch by inch, to the weed forest of the maybe-front-lawn. Zeke's car was still there. I had the keys. In an exhausted stupor I drove back to that town without a name, or at least none that holds importance, and got on a train.

The train ride took two hours. Two hours spent

wiping my newborn, now dead, vomit-baby from every crevice and pore and crease of my body. Two hours spent on the receiving end of stink eyes and horrified gazes. Whispers and rumours and dismay. But I can't blame them. Some things should be observed. Some things should be consumed.

I was a big guy once. Once being two weeks ago. Now I am like Zeke; rotting, deteriorating, little but a skeletal frame wearing a sack of flapping skin, mind wandering, body failing, soul...missing?, perhaps, or just hiding. I talk to myself a lot, talk to the wall, talk to the void in between myself and everything else, talk to the unnamed and unseen people haunting the streets.

I swear I saw him once, but I could have dreamt it, or remembered it wrong, or remembered it right, but on top of a wrong, or either one or none in between. A young boy, maybe eight, maybe eighty, wearing an old-timey depressingly green-brown tweed suit, at least three sizes too large. He might have smiled at me, or frowned, or upside-down-frowned, but I felt nothing, no more, except for that lukewarm acidic bile rising, that nausea that exists on the outside and inside simultaneously, that pill or sometimes capsule she gave me, and then whispered with dancing cobra lips a single word of impregnating malady;

Mdłości.

THE FATHOMLESS DEPTHS

Some days life just doesn't make sense. Some days you just helplessly sink into the fathomless depths of your mind. Some days it feels like an endless loop of misplaced words and bad decisions. A dull and pointless ascetic practice stuck on repeat. Today was a day much like that. I woke up to a grey and formless existence, my mind feeling like amorphous sludge, slowly reshaping all the nonsense into coherent thoughts. Nothing felt real, nothing felt tangible. I guess that's why I called in sick. I just couldn't handle anything but myself today.

I've had these dark moments ever since I was a little girl. My mother had them too. I guess it's hereditary. They come and go without any discernible pattern. It's like a bad wifi connection; you never really know when you're online. Sometimes everything just lags and idles, and your thoughts never really fully loads. And even though you're fully aware of this, you still end up losing your shit. Why now?! you'll shout. Why this exact moment?

The morning went by in a fog of blurry motions and incoherent conversations. We were late. We were always late. That's the one constant in my life; never being on time. I must have rushed them into the car, I can't really remember, but I remember Lorelai complaining the whole ride over. She forgot something. Her lunch? Backpack? There was always something. I don't know, I can't recall. Laurel was silent. She was always like that. Polar-opposite identical twins. Who's bright idea was it to invent those, eh? I swear, some days you just feel like drowning them, you know.

We were five minutes late, maybe more, and the girls jumped out of the car simultaneously. I waved at them before they disappeared beneath the underpass, but they didn't see me. I guess they were in a hurry. I sighed deeply and rested my head on the steering wheel. Even my medication didn't do much on days like these. I just wanted to go home, get in my bed, sleep until everything felt better.

I think I drove for five minutes before I noticed them. At first I just saw a brief movement, like a few strands of blonde hair in my peripheral vision. Then I heard a strange splashing sound, almost like waves hitting the shore. But there was nothing in the rearview mirror. I drove for another five minutes before I heard the giggling.

I almost swerved into oncoming traffic as I felt a hand on my shoulder. It was cold, freezing, and I barely avoided hitting the curb on the other side as I desperately tried to regain control of the car. I hit the brakes full force, and managed to stop inches from a man stumbling drunkenly along the side of the road.

He started yelling and cursing at me madly, but suddenly stopped as his gaze wandered to the back of the car. His eyes widened in fear and he staggered away in a hurry. I checked my rearview again. Still nothing. It's all in my head, I thought. Just one of those days. I turned around slowly.

There they were. Both of them. Sitting in the backseat smiling, holding hands. I looked in the rearview again. Nothing. All in my head, all in my head, all in my head, I kept repeating in my head. I closed my eyes. Opened them. Closed them again. Kept them closed for minutes. Opened them.

"Can we go, please," Lorelai nagged. "We're gonna be late!"

Her voice sounded different. I mean, it was hers, I was sure of it, but it almost sounded like it came from far away, like it echoed through a vast space or something. Her face was pale, and her hair wet and messy, like she'd been out in the rain for hours. How could this be?

"I dropped you off," I mumbled weakly. "I dropped you off at school."

Laurel just sat there smiling, her pale blue eyes fixated on me with unnerving intensity. She looked just like Lorelai, except for those piercing eyes. Same pale face. Same wet, messy hair.

"No you didn't," Lorelai said. "You said we could skip school and go on an adventure today."

Her voice raised and lowered in pitch erratically, and her eyes widened in anger as I sat there trembling and sweating, not quite knowing what to do, or think, or feel. I wanted to get out of the car, run away, hide, because I knew deep down that those things weren't the girls.

"You told us!" Lorelai shouted. "You told us we were in a hurry!"

I yanked the car door handle in a panicked frenzy, but it wouldn't budge. I threw myself over to the passenger side and did the same, but to no avail. It was stuck. I was trapped in there. And Lorelai was getting angry. She had that after my mother. The temper. The darkness. Imagine that. She was named after my mother, Lori, and she essentially became her.

"No, no, no," I muttered to myself. "This isn't happening. This isn't real."

Suddenly I felt icy-cold fingers gripping my throat. Lorelai was suddenly in the front seat, her facial features distorted and hideous. There was no color in her eyes anymore. They were just...white. I felt her fingernails digging deep into my neck as a loathsome smile formed on her pale bluish lips.

"DRIVE!" she shouted loud enough for the rearview mirror to crack.

I pushed the pedal to the metal and the tires screeched discordantly as the car slid onto the highway. Lorelai wasn't in the front seat anymore. She was in the back again, holding Laurel's hand tightly.

"Wh-Where are we going?" I muttered. "I don't know where we're going."

The girls were giggling and playing in the backseat, completely ignoring me. I didn't want to raise my voice. I didn't want to upset them. So I just drove. Drove for hours with those ghastly impostors harrowing in the back. I couldn't see them in the rearview, and I didn't want to turn to face them. But yet I could feel everything they did. I could picture every twitch of a muscle on those lethargic bodies in my mind. I knew they were staring. Staring and smiling.

"Are we almost there?" Lorelai complained. "I'm tired."

I thought I had just been driving around aimlessly, fuelled by horror and fear, but I suddenly realised I knew exactly where we were, which I found extremely odd because I'd never been there before. It was a bleak place. Barren and desolate. A cold and gloomy peninsula, surrounded by the harsh, endless sea. Beyond was nothing but the dark horizon.

"We're here," I said as I pulled the car over by an old pier at the end of the peninsula.

The pier was a dreary, ramshackle mess, barely sturdy enough to carry its own weight. The wood was greying and covered in algae, and it was quite clear that it had been abandoned for decades. There were no signs, no way to identify the place, but I knew its name by heart; Paradise Pier. How on earth could I possibly know that?

"Finally," Lorelai rolled her eyes. She was in the front seat again, her hideous smile now stretching unnaturally from ear to ear. I closed my eyes instinctively as she leaned in to me slowly. I could feel her cold, leathery hands caressing me, stroking my hair. Then I felt pain. Instant, mind-numbing torment. I screamed until I had no air left in my lungs. Anoxia, they call that. It's strange how the mind can just focus on something so utterly absurd in the middle of a trauma. It's called anoxia, absence of oxygen.

When I came to again, Lorelai was gone. I let out a relieved sigh. All in my head, all in my head. But the pier was still there, and it was still so eerily familiar, like a long lost dream.

"You could have stopped her," Laurel said. Her voice sounded horrific, like she was somehow gargling the words into my ears underwater. I turned around in shock. She was still just sitting there, staring at me. The creepy smile was gone however, but it was replaced by something far more disturbing. Her face was bloated. Bloated and blue and horrid.

"You could have saved me, Lorelai," she said. "But you just saved yourself."

Whatever blanket had covered my mind suddenly vanished. I felt a clarity I can't really explain. It was like waking up from a dream within a dream within a dream, realising for the first time you've just been dreaming all along. Realising that everything was a lie.

"I couldn't," I said. "I wasn't strong enough."

My mother didn't drop us off at school. She said we were going on an adventure. She'd been in her dark place for weeks, so we were so happy and excited that she had finally emerged. She drove for hours. We were going to Paradise Pier, she said. It was a wonderful, magical place. Maybe we could even stay there forever.

"You could have," Laurel said.

I was now in the backseat. In my seat. I didn't wear my seatbelt. I didn't like being told what to do. Laurel did, however. She was always silent and obedient and nice. My polar opposite. Tears started filling up my eyes and I just embraced her. Embraced my twin sister.

"I'm so sorry," I murmured. "I was scared. I was so scared."

My mother pulled the car over by the pier. She didn't say anything. Didn't do anything. Just sat there. Staring into the dark horizon. Staring and smiling. Then suddenly, out of nowhere, she just did it. No warning. No explanation. The car screeched discordantly as it accelerated onto the ramshackle pier. Moments later we were all swallowed by the fathomless depths.

"I forgive you," Laurel said softly. "But you have to do something for me."

The car overflowed with water in a manner of seconds. I tried pulling Laurel loose, but her seatbelt was stuck, and I was completely overcome by uncontrollable panic. At some point I just gave up. I stopped thinking about anyone but myself. I was too late to save her. Always too late. I rolled open the window, ignoring Laurels desperate pleas for help, and swam out of the rapidly sinking car.

"Anything," I cried. "I'll do anything for you Laurel."

Laurel smiled. She wasn't bloated and blue and horrid anymore. She was beautiful and colorful and vibrant, just like I remembered her.

"Come join me," Laurel said. "It's so lonely down here."

So here we are. At the end. The twins are still sitting in the backseat. Staring into the dark horizon. Smiling and laughing and holding hands. I'll be signing off now. I just wanted to say goodbye.

I am bound for the fathomless depths.

THE NAMELESS STREET RITUAL

Pancreatic cancer. That's what it's called, the thing that's slowly killing my wife. It doesn't sound so horrifying, does it? Pancreatic? It's the cancer part that's bad, obviously. It's the cancer part that's slowly eating away at my wife, my one true love, relentlessly devouring every part of her, until there's just a withering, wheezing stranger left, her tormented gaze begging for it to be over; every fiber of her being aching for death.

I'd tried everything up to that point. And I mean everything. You'd be amazed, and appalled, at the sheer quantity of bullshit snake oil miracle remedy shit you'll find if you just go looking for them. All the healers, shamans, witch doctors and loathsome charlatans preying on the weak and desperate. But conventional medicine had failed me. Failed my wife. And I couldn't find it in me to give up, no matter how much she begged me to.

At first glance the Nameless Street seemed like just another hoax. A nonsensical ritual pasta designed to amass internet points. But the more I looked into it, the more I came to believe that there had to be some merits to it. Too many identical claims, too many similar experiences, too many vivid descriptions. Coming up empty on all other leads, I decided there'd be no harm in giving it a shot.

The Nameless Street was as simple in its complexity as it was complex in its simplicity. At the end of an unnamed street, look for an abandoned house with a locked basement door. Find a way to get into the basement without breaking the lock. In the room beyond you'll find two chairs facing each other. Make sure to lock the door again. Place sixty-six candles in a wide circle around the room. At the center, place one sixth of a candle. When night is at its darkest, light all the candles. Sit down in the chair with the back turned to the door, and count loudly to sixty-six and one sixth. If you get it all right, the Devil himself will appear, granting you a single wish in exchange for your soul.

Finding the Nameless Street wasn't easy, but at the same time it wasn't that hard either. I just stumbled upon it, I guess. I went searching every evening after my visit at the hospital. That's the only thing that kept me going. Seeing her wasting away; another fragment of her dying every day. Body, mind, soul, soon there'd be nothing left but memories. I paced the streets tirelessly for weeks, making sure to cover as much ground as I possibly could. Then, one night, it was just there.

The doctors gave her a month, maybe less. We'd been together since high school. 10 years. Got married as soon as we legally could, sharing dreams of children, a house, a dog, a station wagon. A normal, boring, wonderful life. We were going to grow old together. Die together, locked in an unbreakable embrace, exhaling our last breath at the exact same moment. But now she was leaving. Fading. And I felt helpless and lost and alone. I needed this. I needed it to be real.

It was just like I'd imagined it. A harrowing house at the end of the street, all the windows smashed in, front door missing, exterior greying and faded. A faint smell of urine lingered inside, and the walls were all covered in tasteless graffiti. I didn't care to inspect the house itself. I was there for one thing. I descended the ramshackle stairs leading down to a surprisingly sturdy looking wooden door, and gave the handle a try.

Locked.

This was the place.

When I wasn't at the hospital, Stan was. I didn't even have to convince him. I just wanted someone to be there by her side at all times, and I think he understood that. My brother got along well with my wife, and it seemed like the right thing to do. When I arrived after work, Stan would be there, and we'd talk for a bit. It affected him too. Devoured him like it devoured me. He looked older than any younger brother should. I had to fix this, or we'd all just fade to nothingness.

I returned the next evening with candles and tools. I had no idea how to pick a lock, but luckily some guy on YouTube did, and after about thirty minutes of finagling and cursing, I heard a soft click, followed by the door sliding open.

The basement was just how I'd imagined it too. Cramped and damp and dark, two chairs placed at the exact center of it. Once I'd made sure the door was locked, I started placing the candles in a wide circle, saving the one sixth of a candle for last.

I sat down on the chair with the back turned to the door, and waited. When the night is at its darkest. How can you tell? Isn't night just a lack of light? When the sun is down, isn't it just down? I felt stupid, ignorant, like I'd fooled myself into believing something that'd never work. How could it work? It was utterly ridiculous. But still, I couldn't give up now. I had to try. I owed my wife that much.

I started lighting the candles. I figured it wouldn't get any darker, and couldn't very well spend all night in that creepy abandoned shithole. Better to just get it over with. It took a good five minutes to get all the candles in the circle lit, and I swallowed deeply before lighting the final one. It didn't feel any different, but I sat down regardless, and started counting loudly to sixty-six and a sixth seconds.

"One, two, three, four." My voice rang hollow and insincere. I glanced around anxiously while counting, but save for the dancing shadows cast by the flickering candles, there was nothing.

"Thirty-three, thirty-four, thirty-fi-"

"Don't you find this hysterically ridiculous?" a cheery voice queried from behind me.

I suppose I wasn't really expecting anything to happen. Not really. Thus the sudden realisation that someone was there, behind me, caused me to tumble off the chair in shock, and I spent quite some time desperately struggling to get back up.

"I mean, you must have stopped at sixty-six and a sixth and gone 'Wow, this is some next level absurd as shit nonsense', right?"

He was not what I expected. At all. He was young, maybe in his mid-twenties, long blonde hair, dressed in jeans and a white hoodie. He smiled widely, emerald eyes sparkling vividly as they scanned the room.

"All you had to do was ask," he mimicked holding a phone up to his ear. "No need for this unnecessarily elaborate…" He paused, waggling his right index finger around theatrically. "I want to say ritual?"

"Wh...Who are you?" I stammered incoherently.

"Such a useless question," he chuckled. "Names have no meaning here."

"Are you…" I staggered back into the wall. "Are you the Devil?"

"Look, buddy," he grinned widely, "It really isn't important. What is important, however, is what I can do for you."

He wandered around the room nonchalantly, eyes darting back and forth between the flickering candles and me. He was tall and slim, yet unnaturally imposing, like he could squish me like a bug at any moment if he felt like it. I kept backing into the wall senselessly like a frightened animal.

"Let's sit, shall we?" he beckoned for me to join him as he sat down. "We have much to discuss."

"Jesus Christ," I mumbled. Was this really happening? Nothing about it felt right. It felt unholy. Blasphemous. My back scraped against the cold protruding bricks of the wall, like the pain somehow grounded me to reality. "Jesus fucking Christ," I added.

"Look, you can call me anything you'd like if it makes you feel better," his piercing eyes dug into mine. "It really doesn't matter what fantasy you subscribe to. In the end they're all nothing but lies, and just like names they only hold meaning to owners and believers. And let's just say I'm neither. Now, please just sit, James. You're making this whole satanic deal thingy very awkward for the both of us."

"How do you know my name?" I mumbled, still subconsciously backing into the unmoving wall.

He threw his head back and laughed heartily. "So you came here ready to summon the literal Devil, but you're surprised he somehow knows your name? James, James, you're really out of your depth here, you know that right?" He motioned towards the vacant chair. "Sit, James. Sit, and we'll discuss what I can do for Nora."

The mention of her name brought me back from whatever delirious state I was in. I suppose I immediately stopped caring whether it was real or not. The end justifies the means, isn't that what they say? Even if I was hallucinating, even if this was some insanely convoluted hoax, I had to give it a shot. I'd never forgive myself if I didn't at least try. I hesitantly stumbled to the chair, and sat down facing the man.

"How do you know her name?" I asked. "How can you possibly know any of this."

"We've been through this, James. I know all I need to know, and that's just how it is. For instance I know that Nora, sweet, sweet darling Nora, is slowly dying from cancer. I say slowly, but that's really not the case anymore, is it? I'd give her maybe a few days, a week at most. Better start making some arrangements. Choose a nice coffin, find a decent plot, organize the service. These things take time, you know. Wouldn't want to half-ass her funeral now, would you?"

I felt a sudden rush of anger. Anger and resentment and sadness and despair. I wanted nothing more than to just punch his infuriatingly carefree face in, but something deep down inside me told me that would be a horrible idea. Instead I just broke down crying. Heavy, convulsive sobs.

"There, there, James my boy. It isn't over yet," he smiled. "What if I told you I could take it all out of her. The cancer. Just reach into that frail, broken body, and rummage around in there until it's all gone. Wouldn't that be something?"

I stared at him blankly, tears running down my face. "Co...Could you do that?" I murmured. "Could you really do that?"

"I could," he leaned back, hands behind his head. "But you know, I'd have to put it somewhere else. Natural order, balance, and all that jazz. But I'll do you a solid, since I kinda like you James."

"Wh...What do you mean?"

"See, what I do with it, the cancer, is entirely up to me. I mean, I could just stuff it in you. And normally I would, you know. I'm a stickler for irony. You know how it goes: you can't live without the love of your life, so you make an unholy deal with some diabolical entity to save her, only to die days later. Hil-arious. But since you've grown on me like a tumour, I'll do you one better. What do you say we stick the big C into your worst enemy instead?"

My worst enemy? Did I even have enemies? I mean, I didn't really like my boss. And my neighbor was incredibly annoying, and truth be told I could really do without the you're-not-good-enough-for-my-daughter attitude from my mother-in-law too. But an enemy? I suppose my co-worker, Eric, was the closest thing I had to an enemy. He was demeaning and malicious, always going out of his way to make me look bad. The more I thought about it, the more I realised just how much I hated him.

"Yes," I said. "Do it. There's this guy, Eric, at my jo-"

"Oh, I'm sorry," he interrupted. "I think you misunderstood me. I don't need to know who you think your worst enemy is. No, James, my guy, I know who your worst enemy is. I just need a 'yes' and the old handshake to confirm our arrangement, that's all."

"How do I know you can do it?" I suddenly felt a

sobering doubt rising. This was all too good to be true. Too fucking crazy to be real. "How do I know I can trust you?"

"I'm glad you asked," he chuckled. "It's smart, you know, to question these things. Sure, I manifested in this locked basement out of thin air, and know more about you and your wife than any random stranger possibly could, but I get it; you need proof."

He stood up from the chair and leaned in close to me. I instinctively sank into my seat, desperately trying to avoid his piercing gaze.

"Now, I would love to say that this wasn't going to hurt," his eyes gleamed eerily in the darkness. "But I'd be lying. And truth is everything, isn't it? That's why you're here. For the truth. You might not know it yet, granted. But you will. And who knows, you might even come to thank me one day."

"What are you tal-"

With inhuman speed he stuck both his hands into my chest. I know it's impossible. Of course I know it's impossible. But the pain was real. And the blood was too. Insufferable pain, like every nerve ending in my body was set on fire. Fountains of blood showered us both, and I felt the sudden presence of an impenetrable darkness.

"Don't cross over just yet, Jamesy boy," he laughed. "We're only just getting started."

I could feel him touching me from the inside, fingers digging into tissue and muscle and organs, every little prod bringing insurmountable waves of torment, somehow spreading to every pain receptor at once. I couldn't breathe, so I couldn't scream, but I imagine every synapse in my body lighting up simultaneously to form a hysterical howl.

"Ah," he licked his lips. "There we go. Just the suckers we were looking for. They can be a handful, let me tell you, and all this blood makes it hard too, you know. Takes practice."

With a forceful yank he pulled his hands back, leaving behind a gaping hole in my chest. I should be dead, I thought as I stared into the mangled depths of my own body. I was convulsing uncontrollably in spasming seizures, but I still managed to get a long, good look at what he was proudly holding in his blood dripping hands.

"Recognize them?" he laughed. "They're called lungs. Primarily used for breathing I've been told. Ugly suckers though, don't you think? Most of the stuff you find on the inside doesn't look as good on the outside. I guess there's some meaning to it, you know. Aesthetics and such."

He waved them around playfully, blood squirting everywhere. Every muscle in my body was spasming violently now, and I felt my mind starting to slip, overwhelmed by the unimaginable pain. I'm going to die, I thought. This is it. This is where they'll find me. But just as the alluring darkness was about to overcome me, I was brought back by his cheery voice.

"So does that do it?" he asked, his mouth now inches from my ear. "Are you convinced? Do we have an agreement?"

I tried my best to nod, but I'm not sure you could easily discern the voluntary movements from the involuntary anymore. Blood was flowing in thick streams from the gaping wound on my chest, pouring into an impossibly deep pond on the cold concrete below. Suddenly he grabbed my hand, and shook it vigorously.

"Good lad," he laughed heartily. "It's a deal then. I'll yank the nasty tumours from sweet darling Nora, and pack your worst enemy full of the stuff. Really can't wait for this one, James, sounds like an absolute riot!"

The darkness was closing in, and I felt some manner of peace as a thick blanket of heavy tiredness enveloped every part of my being.

"I'll be on my merry way then," he said. "People to meet and eat, you know how it goes."

I could hear him walking towards the door. Heavy steps, echoing through the room. Too heavy for his lithe frame. Everything was turning black now, and I suppose I was mere seconds away from passing out and on when his voice brought me back once more.

"Oh, right, I forgot," he chuckled. "You probably need these."

Mind-numbing pain shot through my body as he pushed his hands into the wound again, brutally rummaging around in there for what felt like ages. Then, with a sudden yank, he was out again.

"There you go," he said. "Good as new. Keep

those suckers clean now, you hear? Stay away from cigarettes and huffing asbestos." he laughed. "Anyway, be seeing you, James. I have a feeling we'll talk again real soon."

And with that, he was gone. I was left slumped over my chair, wheezing and spasming for minutes, before realising I was...completely fine. I refused to believe it at first. I examined my chest thoroughly, every inch of it, then turned my attention to the floor. Not a drop of blood. Not so much as a papercut on my chest. It was like it had never happened. But it did, didn't it? The pain was so real, so horribly, gruesomely real. Minutes of excruciating torture that felt like years, and then...nothing?

I didn't stick around to question what had happened. I got out of that basement in a panicky haze, and never looked back. When I got home I immediately collapsed on the couch, and slept for twelve hours straight. I'm sure I would have slept longer, probably days, maybe a week, but I was ripped from my deep slumber by the sound of my phone.

"Yeah?" I mumbled. "Who's this?"

"James!" Stan yelled excitedly. "You're not gonna believe this! It's a fucking miracle!"

A miracle.

Even the doctors agreed. There was just no medical explanation for Nora's sudden recovery. No rational way to describe how the cancer had just vanished. Poof. Not a trace left in her. A miracle, they all agreed. Deep down I knew that wasn't the case, of course. It wasn't miraculous at all. In fact, it was probably the exact opposite. But I didn't care. I was just so happy she was still here, still alive, still breathing. I've never cried like I cried that day. Tears of joy. Who knew such a thing could be real?

Weeks went by, and that night in the basement slowly faded from memory. I guess I just went with it, you know. Pretended it was all some vivid hallucination, brought on by sleep deprivation and desperation and grief. And when Eric didn't get horribly sick and die, like I'd secretly hoped, I just let it all go. Life moved on.

Except it didn't. It all stopped in that basement. Maybe not stopped, but perverted? Grew out of control, like cancerous cells.

My wife sat down with me a month later. We need to talk, she said. I could tell by the look on her face that it wasn't anything good. There were tears, lots of them, crocodile and otherwise, and a pained, guilt-ridden expression. She wanted a divorce, she told me. She'd been seeing another man for quite some time now, but because of the cancer, and her imminent death, she didn't have it in her heart to tell me. But now that she was healthy and had her life back, she wanted to move on. Wanted to find happiness again.

"Who?!" I remember yelling. "Who the fuck is he?!"

"It's...your brother," she sniffled pathetically. "It's Stan."

I suppose my life ended there. Betrayal comes in all shapes and sizes, but from my own brother? My own flesh and blood? It was too much to bear. And I guess I felt it already then. The hate. That seething anger and fury and resentment, consuming every fragment of my existence from thereon out.

She moved out the same day. Packed her shit and went to live with my brother. I sat in the darkness of my trashed living room for days, fueled and fed by nothing but bubbling detestation and loathing and hatred. I wanted to burn him alive. Nail him to the wall. Dig out his eyes with a rusty knife. He was already dead to me, but I wanted him dead to the world too.

My worst enemy.

And then, like clockwork, he got diagnosed with cancer. Pancreatic. Such a beautiful word. Rolls right off the tip of your tongue. Pancreatic. Instant and terminal. My brother died days after they first caught it. It spread faster than anything they'd ever seen, they told me. A reverse miracle of sorts. I cried no tears at the funeral. I don't think I'll ever cry again.

Nora couldn't deal with his death. Her sudden recovery followed by the hope of a new life with a new love, smothered instantly by cruel, hideous irony. She hung herself in Stan's garage a week later. I tried to cry at her funeral, I really did, but it was all empty. Hollow and void. A soulless husk. There was this moment, after they'd lowered her coffin, a brief second of serene silence. No birds, no grieving masses, no wind. Just a perfect moment of tranquility. I could hear him clearly then, in the back of my mind. A cheery chuckle, a hearty laugh.

I have a feeling we'll talk again real soon.

Just like the uncontrollable growth of abnormal cells, the amassing sum of my sins spread to cover every aspect of my existence. There is no miracle, reverse or otherwise, waiting for me at the end of the line. There is no light at the end of the tunnel. There is no end to the tunnel. There is no end.

As I stare into the fathomless depths of my empty void soul, I can only nod and agree.

Real soon.

THE DAY I FELL INTO THE SKY

Casadastraphobia they call it. A fear of falling into the sky. The first time I experienced it I was a little kid, lying on a summery lawn looking up into the clear blue above. I imagine the sensation is much like a reverse vertigo; the sky suddenly coming closer, a feeling as if gravity no longer applies, then the horrifying realisation that you're slowly floating upwards. This is all inside your head, of course. That's what everyone keep telling me anyways.

I had several episodes growing up, some more severe than others, until I finally realised I'd be better off just not looking up into the sky. That's treating the symptom, of course, and not the underlying issue, but at least it kept me grounded, so to speak.

The day I fell into the sky I was sixteen, and madly in love. I remember lying in the park, staring into Sarah Dawson's bright blue eyes, her lovely blonde hair spread out in the grass around her head. I wanted so badly to just move in for the kiss, but I suppose I chickened out, and instead turned my gaze to the clear azure above in embarrassment.

It happened just like it had happened so many times before. My gaze drifted into the endless blue, I felt momentarily detached from reality, the sky lowering, my head spinning, my body suddenly light as a feather. Panic gripped my heart, and I tensed up involuntarily.

And then I fell.

Not slowly, like the other times. No, this time it was exactly like gravity had reversed. I launched into the sky screaming, desperately reaching for anything to grab onto. But there was no use. Within seconds I was was hundreds of yards into the air, and I felt the pressure in my head building rapidly. Breathing soon became impossible, and before my body left the troposphere, I suppose I must have passed out.

I woke up in unimaginable pain. Dread immediately overcame me when I realised I couldn't move. Not a single muscle. Even my eyelids seemed unresponsive, yet I could somehow still see. But I didn't want to see. Scanning my newfound whereabouts was somehow even worse than the pain.

"We got a live one, doc," a man's voice called.

"How are the organs?" a different male voice replied.

"Could use a couple of weeks."

"Put it back under then."

I was suspended in the air. The room was dark, but also bright? Two blurry silhouettes moved around methodically, one of them right in front of me. My eyes darted all around the place frantically, collecting as much information as I possibly could. I tried to scream, but there came no sound. Just horrid echoes in my mind. Close your eyes. Close your eyes damnit.

I don't know why it took me so long to realise. Confusion? Phantom pain? Delirium? The man, the blurry silhouette, poked and prodded me idly; every touch like a million needles inserted directly into my nerve endings. Where are my feet? I thought. Where are my eyelids?

"It's conscious, doc," the hazy figure said.

"So?" a voice echoed. "Put it back under."

"Won't it remember?"

"Does it matter?"

I had no feet. There were no feet. Where are my arms? I was a dangling torso, suspended in the air by horrible, cyst-ridden organic wires, contracting and expanding hideously in a rhythmic fashion. My skin was ashen-grey and covered in scars, the deep gashes dripping with disgusting yellow pus. Why can't I close my eyes?

"Aren't we worried about disrupting it?" the figure asked.

"It will fade," the other voice reasoned, "Fade like a dream. Minor changes, perhaps, but miniscule in detail."

"Overloading pain receptors then," the figure said.

With a swift motion the figure stuck his hand into the lower part of my torso. I felt it, somehow. Metal scraping against tissue. You're not supposed to feel it like that, I think? Have you ever experienced pain so great that your mind simply cannot handle it? Like your synapses are continuously lighting up in pure torment? It was like that, except multiplied endlessly.

"Sleep now," the figure said. "It was just a dream."

Then, without ever closing my eyes, everything suddenly went black.

I woke up screaming. Sarah did her best to calm me down, and she later said I seemed completely out of it. I must have passed out, she explained. Sunstroke most likely. Overheated brain. It took me hours to calm down, the vivid experience from that gruesome nightmare replaying relentlessly in my mind. But it wasn't real. Was it? No, it couldn't have been. Just a very vivid dream, surely. All just a dream.

Sarah carefully caressed my hair, and whispered softly that she loved me. I guess that did it. Grounded me again. I stared into her eyes, and finally found courage to kiss her.

I've always been a sucker for those beautiful deep brown eyes.

SOMETHING NEW UNDER THE SUN

I wake up in pain and anger and confusion. For a moment I don't remember where I am. Who I am. When the fleeting dream sensation passes, and I still remain unsure, panic grips my heart. I fall to the floor, hitting the cold concrete with some force. Too much force. I hear a crack. Feel a crack. Warm, sticky blood forms a comforting pool around my head as I lie there sobbing. There is nothing new under the sun, they used to tell us. Oh, how I wish that was true.

There are things I cannot tell you. Not because I don't want to. Not because they don't want me to. Simply because I cannot remember them. My brain, my memory, is a swiss cheese. Most of it remains intact, but look closer and you'll realise there are holes everywhere. Most days I can function just fine. Most days I remember who I am. But then suddenly there'll be a hole somewhere, and I'll spiral desperately into the unknown abyss.

I remember...

I was stationed at a research facility about 200

nautical miles from..somewhere cold. The coast of Norway perhaps. On all the official documents it's a standard oil rig. In reality it isn't. We pull samples from the ocean floor. Some kind of mineral deposit they're interested in. For what I can't say. Science stuff. Classified information.

There were seven of us on that rig over the holidays. Just a skeleton crew to keep everything operational. Mostly broken old men without families to go home to. That way, at least we got to spend Christmas together, you know. Didn't have to be alone. Didn't have to suffer the loneliness.

But it would have been far better if I was alone.

We only had a single sample to pull, then we basically had the week off. I was the only diver. At least I think I am a diver. I was in the water, that much I remember. I recall the murky water enveloping me, a brief feeling of discomfort and thalassophobia as I sink slowly into the depths. No visibility to speak of, just erratic patterns of particles and indistinctive, amorphous shapes.

I gather the sample quickly. Want back up. Don't feel right. But then something catches my eye, like a reflection. But there is no light. How can something reflect what isn't there? I swim towards it cautiously, realising that there's something buried no deeper than a few inches under the mud. Cylindrical in shape. Silvery in color. Pulsating with radiance. Warm to the touch. I grab it, pull it free, cradle it like a newborn babe.

Moments later I find myself back on the platform. People are yelling at me. I can't understand them at first. Just stand there blinking confusedly.

"WHERE IS HENRIK?!" they keep yelling.

That's right. I wasn't the only diver. We were two. We went down together. But only one of us made it back up. You know, it's strange, I can't even remember him anymore. Not his face, not his voice. In my mind I can only ever see his shadow. A black spot where a person once stood. High-pitched, buzzing static where a voice should have been.

Suddenly I am in the shower. Naked, still cradling the radiant cylinder, the warmth of it resonating almost perfectly with the temperature of the blood pumping through my body. I see the shadow of a man on the other side of the shower curtains. He is saying something. Repeating it over and over. No tone in his voice. Flat and without emotion. Can't quite catch the words.

I am sitting at my desk now. Strange living shadows dancing on the walls. The cylinder pulsates soothingly, shimmering eerily from its position at the center of my room. Bizarre symbols reveal themselves on the perfectly sleek surface, alien and outlandish in nature. It's Magnus. I recognize the shadow.

"Why don't you open it? Why don't you open it? Why don't you open it?" he says.

Suddenly I find myself in the mess hall, the cylinder safely tucked under my sweater. Beardsley is yelling at me. He is military. Probably in charge. I can see the veins in his eyes. Muscles protruding threateningly from his neck in convulsing spasms. A gun in my face, finger on the trigger. Thomas and Magnus skulking in the background. But what is he saying?

"Don't," he snarls, "Don't."

Next I recall standing at the edge of the platform. Ivar has a hand on my shoulder. He is shorter than me. But was he always? His hand leaves a sticky, blackish print on my bare skin. His lips are moving, but they are swollen and disproportioned. His voice is replaced by a sudden gush of blood, yet somehow I can understand him.

"I think you should open it. I think you should open it. I think you should open it," he smiles.

Erik is worried. I'm standing in his room now. His eyes aren't present anymore, he tells me. I can see what he means, but he is wrong. They are still there. A liquid gloop slowly creeping down his face. His skin is bleeding. Blood seeping out of every pore. Oozing rivers of red.

"You have to open it. You have to open it. You have to open it," he whispers hoarsely.

Magnus and Ivar throw the lifeless corpse of Beardsley from the edge of the platform. I am holding the cylinder tightly, the radiating glory almost too much to bear. Beardsley disappears into the depths below, his face frozen in a perpetual expression of torment and fear. A clean, circular hole in his forehead. Thomas grabs me from behind, blood spewing forth from every exposed orifice as he yells into my ear.

"OPEN IT! OPEN IT! OPEN IT!"

I am in my room again. Magnus is facing the corner. I think he is crying. Black liquid oozes from countless virulent wounds, dripping to the stained floor in hypnotizing patterns. Thomas turns to me, his eyes now slowly disappearing into his skull. There is nothing left of his skin, the bare, melting muscles forming a pool around us. His lipless mouth convulses.

"Too late. Too late. Too late."

Ivar can't stop screaming. His face is now one with the floor, bones nothing but a sludgy pulp. He will soon join the others. Soon be at rest. Just a few more hours of unrelenting, mind-numbing pain.

"Make it stop. Make it stop. Make it stop," he sobs.

Next I am wandering the dark hallways, the rough metal surface now smeared with the discolored liquified skin, flesh, bones and organs of my co-workers. The cylinder remains safe under my arm. I know what I have to do. This I remember. A moment of clarity. Order in chaos.

Rough waves below as I reach the edge. Arms outstretched, gripping the cylinder tightly. This can't continue. This has to stop. A single motion then, eyes closed, releasing the burden. Freeing myself.

Next? Lights. Blinding lights, deafening sounds. Helicopters. Men shouting. Many questions. Some I answer, some I can't. My memory is a swiss cheese. Holes everywhere. They carry me away. Fly me over the ocean.

Then I wake up here.

They tell me I'm lucky. A miracle even. By all accounts I should have been a puddle of human sludge just like the others, slowly seeping through the cracks of the platform into the watery depths below. But I am not. I am healing. Slowly, steadily, getting stronger. Holes in my brain closing.

"What did you do? What did you do? What did you do with it?" they ask.

"I dropped it. Back where it belongs. Back into the vast lightless tomb," I lie.

The holes in my mind aren't closing. They're expanding. But something is growing in the gaps. Something not me. Something not of this world. Something that I set free.

Set free when I opened the urn.

I found something new under the sun. And now it is finally emerging.

BLOOD ON THE WALL

"So what do you make of it?" I asked the plumber. Steve, I believe his name was. Plumber Steve.

"Sure as hell looks like blood to me," he said, staring at the rusty red discharge dripping down the wall. "But I'm no biochemist or anything."

My wife had jokingly referred to it as blood, so that's the first thing I told the plumber. You know, as a joke. Hey plumber Steve, we've got a real bad case of the old blood dripping down the walls here, mind taking a look?

"You're kidding right?" I stared at him in disbelief. He seemed like the kind of guy that would think this sort of stuff was funny. You know, stupid.

"I don't know, man," he stroked his chin nonchalantly. "The color checks out, and it has roughly the same texture, wouldn't you say?"

This guy, I thought to myself. I'm not even sure why I called the plumber in the first place. The weird thing was that there weren't any pipes anywhere near the wall in question. I'd gone over every inch of the place, read through all the blueprints, even drilled a hole at the base of the roof. There was simply nothing there.

"Maybe you got a corpse or something up there?" he chuckled nervously. "Have you checked on your wife lately?"

I really do hate bad comedians. They're right up there with people who use whilst instead of while, and people who chew with their mouth open. I just shook my head, and snickered half-heartedly.

"So there's nothing you can do?" I asked.

"Hey man, if there's no pipe or hole or anything I can enter..." he winked suggestively, then shrugged.

I sighed, and thanked him for his service to my basement, which is to say I told him he was useless. He replied with a douchy smirk, and handed me a bill that had me reconsidering my chosen career.

"No luck?" Dasha, my wife, asked.

I shook my head. "I just don't get it," I said. "This shouldn't be fucking rocket surgery."

"I think you mean brain science," she giggled. "But I'll admit, it's pretty damn weird."

We'd only had the house for a little over a week, but I was already regretting buying it. Sure, it was relatively cheap, and who doesn't love a big old mortgage, but there had been nothing but problems with it since we moved in. Lights flickering, drafty spots all over, strange noises in the walls, and then the leak in the basement yesterday to top it all off. And don't even get me started on the neighbors.

"Maybe we should talk to the neighbors?" Dasha suggested, peering out the kitchen window.

"Which one?" I asked. "Let's see, we got the big old weirdo, the demented old crone, the blond surfer guy with a seemingly endless supply of identical white hoodies, oh and let's not forget the creepy middle aged twins."

"Come on," she poked me in the ribs playfully. "Stop being such a grump. I'm sure they're nice people."

I'd managed to dodge them all thus far. I heard someone knocking like crazy on the door once, but I was half asleep from a full night of failing to locate that damned sound in the walls, so I'd buried my head under the pillow and ignored whomever it was. I suppose I couldn't avoid them forever, though. That's not the neighborly thing to do I guess.

"I'm sure," I replied sarcastically. "Hey, shouldn't you be at work?"

"Just heading out now," she kissed me on the cheek. "Love you. Don't go crazy down in that basement, you hear?"

"No promises," I smiled. "But I'll try."

My wife worked wacky shifts. I guess that's what nurses do? I couldn't keep on top of her crazy work schedule half of the time, so I often found myself confused when I woke up and she wasn't there, or when she suddenly came home in the middle of the night. I mostly worked remotely, short term freelance contracts, which basically meant whenever I felt like it. I hadn't been feeling like it since we bought the damned house, which was becoming something of an issue.

"It has to be the foundation, right?" I muttered to myself, bringing my coffee downstairs with me. I was fixated on that wall. And the noises. Couldn't seem to let them go.

The basement was fairly small and cramped, and we were originally going to use it for storage. That's why I had to fix the leak post-haste, lest all our useless crap that we never used would be rendered unusable.

"Maybe rust water?" I suggested, carefully balancing my coffee down the uneven stairs.

I stopped abruptly on the last step, spilling my coffee all over myself. Normally I would have shrieked in a rather unmanly fashion as the burning hot liquid ran down my legs, but in this instance the shock of what I was seeing far outweighed any physical pain.

The wall was squeaky clean. No a single spot on it.

I carefully put down the remnants of my coffee on the stairs, and sauntered over to investigate the impossibility of it, but before I got more than a few steps, the lone light bulb hanging from the ceiling started flickering like crazy, before going completely dark moments later.

"Son of a bitch," I mumbled, stumbling around blindly, knocking over several boxes of god-knows-what.

Ringa-dinga-ding-ding the doorbell suddenly rang from upstairs. I must have knocked over every last thing in that basement in a fit of panic before I finally found the stairs, knocking over my coffee cup in the process. "Fucking shit," I shrieked as the hot coffee spilled all over my feet.

"You alright there fella?" a cheery male voice called from the darkness of the basement.

"Holy shit!" I yelled, instinctively turning toward the sound, which in turn led to me tumbling down the stairs, landing flat on my back.

"You know," a pair of floating, glowing emerald eyes uttered, "I knew the guy who used to live here."

"Who the fuck is there?!" I demanded. "Get the fuck out of my house!"

"I do apologize," the eyes chuckled. "I keep forgetting you lot need light to see."

The light bulb lit up, flickering erratically like a seizuring strobe light, every split second or so illuminating a slender man wearing jeans and a white hoodie. He was grinning widely, his sparkling green eyes darting all over the basement.

"Hey, uh, you're, uh, you're the, uh, surfer, uh, guy, uh, neighbor."

"Spot on," he smiled. "Although I haven't surfed for quite some time. I hope you don't mind, but I figured I'd let myself in, since you seemed rather... preoccupied."

He paced around the room idly, gracefully avoiding all the shit I'd knocked over without even looking. How the hell did he get down here so fast? And how did I not hear him coming down the stairs?

"He hung himself," the man said. "The previous owner. Right over there, see?"

He was pointing to a spot in the corner of the room. I squinted and blinked feverishly, like I somehow expected to see him still dangling there.

"Did you somehow expect him to still be dangling there?" the man chuckled. "I'm sorry, you'll just have to take my word for it."

I sat up uncomfortably, my back digging into the lower steps of the stairs. I couldn't think of anything to say. What do you say to a person who manifests out of thin air in your basement?

"Can you maybe fix the light?" I said, shielding my eyes from the seizure-inducing blinking.

The man laughed, and slapped his forehead theatrically. "Why, of course. I always forget these silly little things." He snapped his fingers, and the light instantly stabilized. I swallowed deeply as his gleaming green gaze settled on me.

"I'm here about your plumbing, so to speak," he said, pointing to the wall. "I've been told you've been having some issues with blood flooding your basement? You know the stuff, right? Thick, crimson liquid, usually confined to the inside of a body? (Nine out of ten doctors will tell you that having it on the outside is a classic symptom of you dying a horrible death)."

"Uh," I said. "Yeah, I mean, it's not blood, that was just a joke. And it's not there now, so I guess it's fixed?"

"Are you sure?" he asked, grinning widely. "Maybe you should take another look."

I glanced at the wall in question, and let out another rather umanly shriek as I realised it was literally covered in deep red oozing sludge, flowing incessantly from a single point close to the ceiling, all the way down to the floor.

"That's at least a couple of gallons worth," the man said, stroking his chin. "Quite the mess. Should see a plumber about that."

I edged back against the stairs. "Isn't…Isn't that why you're here?" I asked.

"Oh yeah, you're right," he threw his head back and laughed. "I'm here to remind you."

"Re…remind me of what?" I murmured.

"That you already know where it comes from, fella. You've always known. Just takes some digging is all. You keep locking it away."

"I…I don't understand."

"Oh, you will," he grinned, his emerald eyes burrowing into mine. "Come on buddy, let's go see your wife. She'll show you."

He sauntered past me, and beckoned for me to follow him as he started ascending the stairs. "You coming or what?" he asked. "I haven't got all damned day."

"My wife…Dasha," I said, shifting restlessly. "She's at work."

The man shrugged and smiled. "You sure about that?" he said. "You sure she didn't come home while you were sleeping?"

Sleeping? No, it was midday wasn't it? The

plumber came around noon, and Dasha left for work an hour or so later. There was no way in hell I'd spent that long in the basement.

"Ah, I see what's going on," the man slapped his forehead again. "It's the temporal thingy messing with you. Yeah, it'll do that sometimes. Some algorithmic snafu or other. I need to talk to the engineers about that."

"What in damnation are you on about?" I said. "Temporal thingy?"

He laughed again. A long hearty laugh. "Nicely put, Wolfgang," he said. "But it's easier if I just show you."

He put his hands into his pockets, and whistled cheerily as he quickly skipped up the remaining steps, disappearing through the door moments later. "Last call," he yelled. "I'm a busy man. Got places to burn, people to eat, you know how it is."

I sat for a while in the dim light, desperately trying to make sense of the situation. There was no such thing as sense, of course. Everything that had happened since the plumber left defied all logic and reason. But somehow it all seemed so...familiar, like I'd seen it happen before. I sighed deeply, and followed him up to the first floor.

"There you are, Wolfie-boy," he grinned as I emerged through the door. "I was just about to call off our arrangement, but I'm glad you came to your senses, as it were."

"Arrangement?" I asked, staring up at the impossibly imposing figure before me.

"Come on," he said, and gave me a pat on the back. I shuddered as the freezing cold fingers dug into my flesh, if only for a brief moment. "A trip down memory lane is required."

I followed him through the kitchen and into the hallway, momentarily losing focus when I noticed how utterly dark it was outside, then regaining it again when I spotted the massive hole in the wall just outside the living room. I stood in absolute silence, just staring at it. It wasn't there before, was it? No, definitely not. I would have remembered a man-sized hole in the wall, surely. That's not something you just forget.

"You couldn't figure it out, could you?" he said, peering into the hole. "Where the sounds came from? Rats in the walls? Wolves in the walls? Couldn't sleep, couldn't eat, couldn't leave it alone. Just had to fix it."

"No, that's…" I said, blinking erratically. "That's not what happened. That's not true."

"Sure it is, Wolfie. Sure it is," he said darkly, staring at me. "You went all looney tunes when you couldn't eat your cereal in peace, and tore into the wall with a sledgehammer. I mean, I get it; breakfast is the most important meal of the day after all."

"No, I didn't," I edged back confusedly. "I mean, I can't remember, I can't…"

"The thing is, Wolfie," he said. "It's dangerous to tear down walls when you don't know what you're doing. Some of those suckers are load-bearing, you know. Sure, it might be structurally sound for a little while, but imagine your wife coming home in the dead of night, all tired and grumpy from a long strenuous shift, then she notices there's a giant flipping hole in the wall, and she's all like 'what in everlasting damnation has Wolfie been up to now', and pops in there for a quick gander, bumps into the wrong thing, and then... BOOM! The roof suddenly collapses on her squishy body, splitting her skull open like a ripe melon, blood steadily flowing into a pool in the corner, slowly seeping down, down, down. Ugh! Man! Wouldn't that be something?"

I swallowed deeply, tears manifesting in my eyes out of nowhere, my hands trembling like crisp autumn leaves, heart pounding out of my chest.

"N...No," I murmured weakly. "It can't...That's not what happened."

The man snickered, and pointed to the hole. "Just one way to find out, Wolfie-boy," he said. "Just a quick look, and then we can talk."

It only took a moment for me to peer into the hole, but it was the longest moment of my life. Dust swirled in hypnotizing patterns within the small, cramped hole, and in the corner I could see a massive pile of rubble, bricks, boards, nails, girders, a pair of unnaturally pale feet sticking out, wearing Dasha's shoes that I got her for her birthday the year they were on sale, so cheap, half price, and the blood, oh my god, the blood, so much blood, oceans of it splitting off into creeks, rivers, fjords, all leading to the corner, seeping down, down, down...

"No!" I cried. "Dasha! No, please god, no, no, no, no."

I don't know why, but I started clearing the debris, diving into the pile, throwing stones and bricks and boards every which way. She was long dead, every last part of me knew that, but it didn't matter, doesn't matter, you have to be sure, gotta be sure, can't let there be doubt, it's my fault, my fault, my god, oh no, Dasha, it's all my fault.

"It is your fault," the man chuckled. "That's how these things usually go, Wolfie-boy. Guilt, despair, damnation, anguish, all the sweet emotions you mistake for love. It's not love, Wolfgang, it's self-preservation. You lot can't handle the pain, so you come to me for the absolute solution. You come to me for absolution."

"Shut up!" I yelled. "Shut up, shut up, shut up."

"Excuse me," he held up his hands dramatically. "Just spittin' the truth over here, didn't mean anything by it. Let me know when you're ready to talk about our arrangement."

I collapsed in the pile, sobbing inconsolably. "Arrangement?" I sniffed. "What do you mean?"

He laughed heartily. "Wolfgang, Wolfgang, how have you not caught on yet? I'm a deal maker by trade, surely you've gathered that much by now."

"You mean," I dried my tears, and stared at him. "You mean you can save her?"

"Oh, I do apologize," he said, grinning widely. "You still seem to be under the impression that this is the first time we're having this conversation. That one is on me, Wolfie-boy. Temporal snafu and all."

"What do you mean!" I yelled hysterically. "Can you just fucking tell me already!"

He crouched down in front of me. "This isn't our first talk, Wolfgang," he said. "In fact, I've lost count, but I'm guessing we're up to hundreds by now. It always ends the same, but I do like to check up on my clients, you know, in case they're experiencing dealer's regret."

"What talk?" I whispered. "What are you offering me?"

He laughed again. "Your wife, sweet, perfect Dasha, of course. I can give her back, just like that," he snapped his fingers. "But there's a catch. Always a catch."

I sat up, meeting his unflinching gaze. "What?" I asked. "My soul? You want my soul? Just take it!"

"Whatever would I do with that?" he chuckled.

"Then what?!" I yelled. "What do you want?!"

"It's real simple," he said. "You can have this glimpse of her. The few minutes every morning, before she leaves for work. That's all. Some back and forth banter, a kiss on the cheek, then goodbye. Then you'll wake up, discovering her body all mashed up to sludgy corpse juice. Go through all that again. All the horror, all the guilt, all the pain, all the suffering. All that for five minutes of her. Hardly seems worth it, does it?"

I nodded weakly. "It is worth it," I said. "It will

always be worth it."

"Well then," he grinned. "Who am I to stand in the way of perpetual self-inflicted torment?"

He grabbed my hand and shook it vigorously. "I'll see you tomorrow, Wolfie-boy," he said. "Always a pleasure."

He disappeared out the hole without a sound, leaving me a sobbing, convulsing mess on top of the crushed corpse of my wife, my sweet, perfect Dasha. I'll never let you go. I'll always choose the agony. There is no compromise, no option, no other way.

Before I go back, before I lose myself, I have to remind myself, have to remember, always remember, never let it go, never let her go…

It is worth it.

It is worth it.

It is worth

THE PALE FACELESS DANCER

I've seen her five times, and every time someone I know ended up dead within hours. I say her, but I'm really not sure if that's even remotely accurate. She has the graceful, elegant, limber movements of a woman, and even though her physique is completely androgynous in nature, I still feel more comfortable imagining her as a woman for some reason.

The first time I saw her I had to be around five or six. The ritual is always the same; I wake up in the pitch-blackness, unable to move a muscle. Then a slowly growing pale pulsating cyst will appear in the periphery of my vision, eventually birthing the dancer in violent, horrible contractions.

She will climb out, pale, tall and spindly, completely hairless. But what really disturbs me is the face. Or lack thereof. I can sort of see the cavities under the thin skin; the flickering movement of her eyes under there, or the way she opens and closes her veiled mouth.

She will stand there in the periphery for a while,

gently swaying side to side, before she starts dancing. I guess the closest I can come to describe it would be a disturbing version of ballroom dancing. She moves gracefully, mimicking holding her partner, gently floating back and forth, her head constantly turned in my direction. I can see her mouth moving under that pale translucent skin, like she's trying to tell me something. But she never makes a sound.

When the unheard music stops, she will too. She would have moved across the room now, usually standing by an exit, either a window or a door. She will continue to move her unseen mouth for a little while, before she slowly fades and becomes one with the darkness. At this point I can choose to wake up. I've only done it twice, the very first time it happened, and the last time it happened.

It's not that something horrible happened that first time I woke up. I think it was more the feeling that she hadn't really left. That she was still there somehow, unseen. Hidden just beyond the veil. My heart wouldn't stop pounding. So I climbed back into bed, and hid under the covers, shaking and crying.

The next morning we got word that our neighbor had passed away. She was a sweet, old lady, Mrs. Barrow. Died of a heart attack. They said she went peacefully, but I'm not so sure about that anymore.

I didn't make the connection back then. How could I? I was barely old enough to understand the finality of death, let alone tie it to a pale faceless nightmare.

But then it happened again. Five years later. The same ritual, the same faceless creature, the same dance. I didn't wake up this time, however. I just slipped back into the comforting warm darkness of sleep.

And I woke up to my mom crying. My grandmother had died. They didn't tell me how until a few years later. She'd drowned in her bathtub. Fallen asleep or had an episode or something. Just collapsed and drowned.

Two years later my uncle died after I was visited by the faceless dancer. Car accident. Must have fallen asleep at the wheel. His body was crushed, mangled, unrecognizable. They had to pick up pieces of him for days. Horrible thing.

Now I was old enough though. Old enough to spot the pattern. To question what the faceless dancer really represented. Was it death? A portent of doom, an omen of unrest? Or something else? Something vile and sinister? A horrible, taunting defiler? Or was it just a messenger? Merely a bringer of bad news? I didn't know, and I didn't really care to know.

When I was seventeen I saw her for the fourth time. This time the dance seemed more intense, more violent, like the unheard music moved in sudden bursts of extreme rhythms. Her face remained still, however, even when her body warped and twisted and turned, the face was motionless, fixated on me.

I woke up crying, trembling, dreading the news I knew was coming. My mom was hysterical, torn up, in shambles. My dad had died on his way home from a business trip. His plane had some technical problems, and had to make an emergency landing. When the cabin crew went around to check if everyone was alright, they found my father dead. He'd somehow got entangled in the seat belt, suffocating as the plane made its unplanned landing. It was ruled a freak accident.

Look, I know what you're thinking. Well, I know what half of you are thinking. Why don't I tell someone? Why I don't I warn them? Do something?

Short answer is I've tried. I've tried to tell someone. But they always look at me like I'm either delusional, or some sick freak. I've lost friends because of it. My mom refused to listen to me, and more or less disowned me when I told her about it. No one will take me seriously.

And I don't blame them. For the longest while, I didn't even believe it. Just some crazy hallucination caused by sleep paralysis or something. The deaths? Coincidences. Nothing more.

I convinced myself of this. And it worked too. For fifteen years.. Never saw her. Never felt her. It was all in my head, some shitty psychotic episode or mental breakdown or something. I was free.

Until a week ago.

It started like all the other times. A pulsating pale cyst, leathery and disgusting, throbbing in the periphery. Then she clawed her way out, following the repulsive rhythms of the contractions. She climbed out slowly, rose to her spindly feet. Stood there swaying side to side. Started the graceful dance, her face always fixated on me. Back and forth, back and forth, her skin-covered mouth moving, forming unheard sentences. She elegantly made her way across the room, and slowly faded away.

But I wouldn't have it. Not this time. No one was gonna die because of me ever again.

My husband was sound asleep next to me. I'd never told him about the pale dancer. And I never will. My kids were in the next room. Noah and Trinity. I couldn't risk them. I couldn't risk her hurting any of them. So I forced myself awake. Trembling and sweating, I got up and slowly crept to the last place I'd seen her; the door.

I don't know quite how to explain it, but there was this residual presence, like an echo of her being. It lingered wherever she'd physically been present, but I felt it stronger where I had last seen her. I opened the door, and slowly made my way to the kids room. I didn't feel her there. But she was close.

I turned around, and immediately let out a hoarse whimper, and stumbled back in shock.

She was there. At the end of the hallway. Still dancing, still moving, still mouthing soundlessly towards me. Then she suddenly disappeared around the corner. I swallowed deeply and thought for a second about waking up John, my husband. But I still couldn't risk it. This was something I had to face alone. So I followed her.

When I turned the corner, she was halfway down the stairs. Her face was still following me wherever she turned, always fixated on me. My heart was pounding, I was sweating and trembling like a leaf, my mind filled with all the potential gruesome conclusions to this horrendous game of cat and mouse. But I had to know. Know what it meant.

So I kept following her. Down the stairs, into the living room, out into the hallway. And then she stopped. She'd reached the door, and just stood there completely motionless. Her mouth wasn't moving anymore either. It was like she was frozen in place.

Then she faded again.

Without thinking I fumbled open the lock, and threw open the door. She was still there. Now standing in the middle of the street. She was dancing again, but in jarring, erratic fashion, her limbs completely out of sync, her head bending in extreme, unnatural angles.

"Stop it!" I suddenly yelled hysterically.

She stopped. Just like that. I moved closer to her, stepped out the door. Over the threshold. And as soon as my body had left the house, she was standing right behind me. I could feel her cold breath on my neck, her spindly hands on my shoulders. I turned around in shock. And I screamed.

Her mouth was open. A bloody, gaping wound, the fleshly skin flapping disgustingly as her hoarse, croaking voice penetrated my ears.

"Thank you," she whispered. "Thank you for leaving."

She stepped into the house and the door slammed shut. I freaked out. Completely lost it. The door wouldn't budge and I couldn't even imagine what was going on in there. Who she was taking from me this time. I banged and clawed and kicked the door, before I finally came to my senses, found a rock, and threw it through one of the windows. The glass shattered instantly, the shards spreading everywhere. I cut myself badly as I clumsily stepped through it.

I raced up the stairs. I've never felt fear like that. Never. The mere thought of anyone hurting my kids sent tremors of terror, horror, rage and sadness, all mixed into a hurricane of unending distress. I more or less kicked the kids door open, only to find both of them sound asleep.

Then I heard the screams coming from my bedroom. Our bedroom. Bestial screams. Screams of utter torment.

"NO!" I yelled as I stumbled down the hallway and into our bedroom.

She was perched atop my husband. Her face still turned to me. But this time she had a horrible, fleshly, bloody smile on that otherwise featureless visage.

"Thank you," she whispered hoarsely.

Then she faded. Gone in an instant. Vanished.

John's eyes were bulging out, his tongue swollen and blue, sticking out between his clenched teeth. His face was purple, but soon turned pale and lifeless. They say he went quickly. But I know better. I know the endless torment he must have endured.

Brain aneurysm they told me. Could happen to anyone. Bad luck.

There's no such thing as bad luck around me.
Only the pale faceless dancer.
And the promise of death.

HANK'S COUNTRY FOOD FAIR

My friend Hank's annual Country Food Fair always draws in the wrong crowd. I have been telling him this for years, but he refuses to listen.

I first started conversing with Hank after reading one of his posts on a cooking subreddit some years ago. We had a lot of things in common and we'd spend hours discussing the finer arts of eclectic cuisine. He told me about the idea he had for the Country Food Fair, and I must admit it sounded interesting, albeit not up my personal alley.

He had been trying to get me to come for years. I've always declined because of the distance, but this year I was in a neighboring town, so I figured I'd pop by and check it out. It was only an hours drive, so it really couldn't hurt.

He hosted the fair on a remote farm about thirty minutes off the main road. Real rustic area, not really my cup of tea, but out of respect for Hank I ignored that obvious lack of elegance. I pulled up around midday, the blistering hot sun making me quite uncomfortable.

I'm a northern girl; too much sunlight can really ruin my day.

There were about ten or so cars there when I pulled up, and it only took seconds before I saw the lumbering figure of Hank jogging down from one of the food stalls. He raised a hand in greeting as I got out of the car and smiled. He really was the sweetest guy.

"Rosie!" he yelled excitedly. "So good to see you!"

He gave me a big old bear hug, and I felt my back cracking as he lifted me off the ground. I let out an audible grunt of pain. "Oh," he said worried, "Did I hurt you?"

"It's fine," I smiled. "Just some back-issues is all. You know how work can be sometimes."

He nodded and ushered me along up the trail to the house. "Don't I just," he said.

The house was the perfect representation of what I had always jokingly referred to Hank as; huge and tasteless. But it did have its rural charm, I'll give it that. Hank offered me some ice tea, and we just sat and chit-chatted for a while, updating each other on life in general. After a while he asked me if I wanted to take a tour of the fair. I was hesitant still, but quietly agreed.

He showed me all the assorted dried meat hung on display, being poked and prodded by other visitors, and albeit conceptually interesting, I just wasn't that into it. It all felt a bit tacky. I think Hank caught on to my general lackluster demeanor, and nudged me jokingly.

"Not your thing, eh?" he asked. "I know you think it's too, what's the word, unsophisticated."

"It's not just that," I said, eyeing the fresh human torso hanging from one of the stalls.

"I just think it's an easy way to get caught."

ME, MIZELL, AND INSPECTOR HOLE-IN-THE-FACE

Having an imaginary friend is quite common I've been told. It's usually a symptom of developing social intelligence, or in some cases having to deal with loneliness and isolation or trauma. All valid and understandable reasons. And sure, there weren't that many kids where I grew up, but even so I still had my best friend Mizell right around the corner, so I never really felt alone in any significant capacity. So why then, might you ask, would I need an imaginary friend?

There's no easy answer, but it all began and ended with Mizell.

Mizell and I were cut from the same cloth. Two peas in a pod. All the wonderful banalities wrapped together to form a magical friendship; inseparable, adventurous, wild, and unhinged. During summer break he'd be at my doorstep the moment I woke up, and we'd spend the long warm hours in the Old Haunted Quarry, or in the Far-Away Forest, or throwing pine cones down the Abyssal Ravine, until the day turned to dusk, and we'd find ourselves laughing and chasing each other home, desperately trying to outrun the creeping darkness, haunted in our vivid imagination by monsters, ghouls, and ghosts at our heels.

These were beautiful times, and I'm sure you remember them yourself. There were no worries, no responsibilities, no dark thoughts; just endless days of mystery and joy, seamlessly overlapping each other until school suddenly started, and the world became grey and monotonous once more.

But the summer I met Inspector Hole-in-the-Face was different. It was darker, colder, shorter, like nature itself tried to warn us about the black days ahead. Mizell and I didn't care, though. Come wind or rain; you'd find us roaming the countryside, hand in hand as we explored every nook and cranny of our quaint little corner of the world.

I still remember the day I met the Inspector vividly. We were fishing for snakes in the Putrid Pond (we'd always come up with silly names for newly discovered places), a blackish-green algae-infested cesspool, and we were debating whether or not snakes actually lived in the murky depths of it.

"Sure they do," Mizell said, his fishing rod flailing wildly about. "They love places like this. Slimy and dark, and with plenty of insects and frogs and stuff to eat. I bet there's a huge one at the bottom, like an enormous sea serpent just sleeping down there."

"Shut up," I laughed. "Look at the size of this thing. It can barely fit the two of us."

"I'm telling you, Sarah," he smiled slyly. "That's how sea serpents are made. They sleep at the bottom of ponds like this, and come up for a snack at night, then tunnel through the earth and into lakes when they get too big. Like that movie, Tremors."

"You're so full of it," I punched him in the shoulder.

"Full of the Truth," he chuckled.

A rustle in some leaves on the other side of the pond drew my attention, followed by the unmistakable sound of twigs snapping. I briefly spotted a shadow disappearing between the trees further into the vastness of the Far-Away Forest.

"Did you see that?" I whispered.

"See what?" Mizell peered at me quizzically. "Did you spot a snake?"

"No," I squinted into the shadowy myriads of trees. "There was something in the forest."

"Oh!" Mizell exclaimed. "It's probably a Chupacabra. They usually eat young sea serpents, you know."

"They do not," I feigned my best you're-so-full-of-it expression. "You're making it up."

"Doesn't mean it's not true," he grinned.

We packed up our stuff and hustled down the trail once we noticed the sun was in descent. We were always late, and we never learned, nor cared. Our parents didn't mind us staying out late, as long as we got home before dark, and we usually beat the darkness by about five minutes give or take.

"I'm telling you," Mizell said in between huffing exhaustedly, "They like the taste of kids. That's why there are so many of them around our school."

He was sharing his hypothesis that all old people are secretly cannibals again, and I was getting tired of rolling my eyes at him.

"You don't think it's because there's a retirement home right next to our school?" I asked mockingly.

"Yes, of course," he shrugged. "But why do you think they built it there, of all places? Heed my advice, Sarah; never trust old peo-"

Mizell suddenly stopped and grabbed onto my arm, eyes wide with fear. For a moment I thought he was kidding, but then I saw the figure approaching us from further down the trail.

"Well, if it isn't Sarah Freakerson," Freddy Purcell taunted, a stupid grin resting on his pimpled face. "You're a long way from home."

Freddy was a couple of years older than me, and a relentless bully. Over the last couple of years he'd started targeting me in particular, and I was getting really fed up with it. Mizell said it was because he had a crush on me. That's how boys show it, he told me. By being mean. I always found that theory utterly ridiculous.

"Real inventive, Freddy," I rolled my eyes. "Doesn't even make sense. My last name is Paulson."

Mizell was slowly inching behind me. He was tiny for his age, only reaching to my shoulders, and that fact in combination with his fiery red hair and numerous freckles made him a prime target for bullies, as he'd state it.

"How's your brother doing, Freakerson," Freddy spat angrily. "Still dead?"

I felt a sudden urge to gouge out his eyes and spit in his empty eye sockets, tear out his tongue, and feed it to him, and I suppose Mizell must have sensed that I was about to lose it.

"Screw you, Purcell," Mizell yelled from behind the comfort of my back. "Everyone knows your father beats you up because you wet your bed."

He really shouldn't have said that. It wasn't a lie; everyone did know that. But everyone also knew that you shouldn't piss off Freddy Purcell. At least not when you're facing him alone in the middle of the woods.

"What did you say?" Freddy snarled, pacing up the trail menacingly.

Mizell knew he'd screwed up, and in an attempt to appear chivalrous he scurried infront of me, shielding me from potential harm. Not that it did any good; Freddy threw him aside like he wasn't even there, and a moment later I was on the ground, the air knocked out of me by Freddy's gut punch.

"That'll teach you," Freddy said, spitting on the ground.

A rustle in the leaves pulled my eyes away from

him. If I weren't more or less incapacitated, lungs still struggling to catch up, I would have screamed as I stared into the hollow crevice of Inspector Hole-in-the-Face's face. He was just there for a split second, but that image is still etched into my retina; a gaunt figure peering at us behind a tree, the gaping chasm in the middle of his face like a perpetual abyss staring back at me.

"Stay away from my part of forest, Freakerson," Freddy said. "Or I'll really mess you up next time."

He kicked some dirt in my face, and stomped down the trail laughing. When I looked back at the bush, Inspector Hole-in-the-Face was gone. I lay there coughing for minutes, Mizell desperately trying to lift me back on to my feet.

"Did you see him?" I murmured at last. "Did you see him in the forest?"

"See what?" Mizell gave me a perplexed stare. "The Chupacabra?"

Mizell helped me get home to the best of his ability, but we couldn't beat the darkness this time around. On the way down I told him what I'd seen in that bush, and I could immediately tell that he didn't believe me. He didn't outright say it, but it was readily apparent if you knew his face.

"It's true!" I demanded. "A man with a hole in his face!"

"I believe you, Sarah," he lied. "It's just, it was so dark, how can you be sure?"

"I'm sure," I pouted. "I know what I saw."

He nodded hesitantly, and embraced me in a long hug. It was our usual bedtime routine, but there was never anything romantic about it, even though I did keep a photo of him on my nightstand. We were friends. Best friends. As close as you can get. An unbreakable bond, destined to remain intact until the end of our days.

Or so I thought anyway.

I didn't sleep very well that night, the vivid image of Inspector Hole-in-the-Face always haunting the periphery of my dreams. I got up around 2 in the morning, and drew his face to the best of my ability. "Did I really see him?", I kept asking myself, staring at the drawing. Or was it just a figment of my imagination?

Mizell was on my doorstep when I woke up as usual, but I guess he must have noticed that I was a bit tired and grumpy, because he was uncharacteristically careful in his approach.

"Let's go to the quarry today," he said matter-of-factly. "Purcell doesn't know about the Stone Hut."

"Yeah, sure," I said, trudging along absentmindedly.

"Hey, Sarah?" Mizell gave me a concerned look. "About the whole thing with your brother…"

We didn't talk about my brother. No one talked about my brother. He was five years older than me, and had died two years earlier in a car accident. What was so weird was that everyone, everyone, seemed to pretend like it had never happened. I didn't understand that. Why would they want to forget him?

"It's fine," I feigned a smile. "Forget it. Freddy's a total moron anyway."

I punched him in the shoulder hard enough for him to wince, and we ran laughing all the way up to the Old Haunted Quarry, whatever worries on our minds now all but faded memories.

The quarry had been abandoned for as long as I could remember, thus nature had claimed most of it back, but the Stone Hut remained; a formation of massive boulders placed haphazardly to form a small cave-like hole underneath. Mizell found it last summer, and we'd come up here every once in a while to drop off supplies and decorate our makeshift base of operations. We had a couple of lawn chairs, a ramshackle wooden table, some cans of soda, a stack of old comics, assorted snacks, and a radio that never worked because Mizell always forgot to bring batteries for it.

"Did you remember to bring batteries this time?" I asked mockingly.

"Shucks," Mizell chuckled, slapping his forehead theatrically. "I always forget."

We messed around in the Stone Hut for hours, drawing maps on the stone walls with sticks, planning our next expedition, pigging out on snacks, before slumping down in our chairs for a brief rest, enjoying the silence of the place. It didn't take long before I heard the sound of him. Vague at first, like it was miles away. Then louder and louder until I was convinced it was right outside the Hut.

"Do you hear that?" I whispered. "What is that?"

I had a hard time trying to identify the sound, but it was eerily familiar; varying between a long, metallic screech, discordant and unpleasant, and a softer creaking noise, like a door on rusty hinges slowly opening.

"Hear what?" Mizell shrugged. "The Chupacabra?"

"Seriously?" I gave him a stern look. "You don't hear that?"

It wasn't deafening, but it was loud enough to echo through our Hut. How could he not hear it? I shushed him, and quietly slipped out, sneaking stealthily between overgrown boulders of all shapes and sizes, until I suddenly found myself face to face with the macabre shape of Inspector Hole-in-the-Face.

He was standing at the end of a long corridor of boulders, his harrowing figure at least twice my size. He was dressed in nothing but brown and green rags, dirty and faded, and for the longest while he just stood there motionless, the impossible depth of the hole in his face like a swirling maelstrom. I couldn't move, eyes lost in the abyss of it, heart pounding ever more frantically. Mizell soon joined me, tugging gently at my sleeve.

"What's going on?" he asked calmly. "What are you doing?"

"Don't you see him?" I whispered, pointing at the

figure.

"Stop fooling around, Sarah," he peered at me quizzically. "There's nothing there."

The bizarre statement brought me out of my trance, and with trembling hands I grabbed Mizell's sweater, pulling him close. His eyes widened in shock. I never laid hands on him. Not like that. This wasn't me. This wasn't Sarah.

"What do you mean?" I snarled furiously, spit flying everywhere. "He's right there!"

Inspector Hole-in-the-Face still hadn't moved an inch, his terrifying frame omnipresent in the labyrinthine network of boulders. I felt like running. I felt like screaming. But even more so I felt like getting some answers.

"Please stop, Sarah," Mizell whimpered. "You're scaring me."

I released my grip on his sweater, and he backed away from me nervously. I wiped sweat and tears from my eyes, and turned my gaze to the Inspector once more. With slow, meticulous steps I inched toward him, biting my lip so hard that I started bleeding. He still wasn't moving, and I'm not sure if that made him less scary, or more so.

"He's right there," I muttered. "Right there."

But then, moments before I reached the Inspector, Mizell came running from behind, throwing himself in front of me.

"Where is he?!" he shouted, flailing his arms around wildly. "Where is the bastard?!"

I froze again, my mind racing as I tried to make sense of the absurdity of the situation. I opened my mouth to speak, but I couldn't think of anything to say. Mizell kept swinging his arms around, most of the hits not only hitting the Inspector, but...going right through him. In fact, Mizell was standing inside the Inspector as he threw the punches.

With a trembling hand I reached out to touch him and...did. His skin was rough, leathery, and cold to the touch, but undoubtedly real. I shuddered, and quickly withdrew.

"You're..." I started, blinking rapidly. "You're standing inside him."

Mizell looked at me, and I could see a smile slowly manifesting on his ridiculous face. Before long he erupted in hysterical laughter, doubling over as he seemingly lost control of his body.

"What are you laughing about?" I demanded. "He is real. I can touch him. I can feel him."

"It's an imaginary friend," he said in between convulsing fits of laughter. "You have an imaginary friend, Sarah."

"Either that," I eyed Inspector Hole-in-the-Face suspiciously. "Or a ghost only I can see."

Mizell suddenly stopped laughing. "I hadn't even considered that," he said, backing away slowly, then turning to me a gleeful grin on his face. "But that's even cooler!"

It was Mizell who decided we should name him Inspector Hole-in-the-Face. The Hole-in-the-Face part was fairly obvious, but the Inspector part took a few days to manifest. The Inspector would show up daily, his horrifying presence announced by the rising, discordant sound of a metal scraping against metal, or the slow creaking of a door opening. He'd always show us something. Or show me something, rather, and he always hovered around us until we solved his riddle.

"He wants us to investigate," Mizell said. "Like he's an Inspector or something."

When he showed up, he'd always be standing next to something he wanted us to look at. It could be simple things, like a headless doll, or a hammer head, a toy car missing its wheels, or a toy soldier without a weapon. He'd point at it, and follow us around until we found the clues he'd left us, then disappear into the Far-Away Forest once we'd completed the task. Usually a completed task just meant making something whole again.

"It's like a puzzle," Mizell theorized. "He wants us to finish a puzzle."

I always wondered how Mizell could take it so lightly. He couldn't see Inspector Hole-in-the-Face, nor touch him, but the objects, the puzzles, were physical even to him. When I asked him about it, he just shrugged, and smiled.

"I know it's probably just you leaving them out

there," he said. "But I don't care. It's fun all the same."

This went on for a week or so, and even though I was perpetually haunted by the gruesome sight of the Inspector, it was the most magical week of my life. Mizell and I loved the enigmatic mystery of the puzzles, and we quickly became lost in the strangeness of Inspector Hole-in-the-Face's obscure games. It was like opening a door to another world; a world where simple household items meant something more, like they were all essential parts of an ever evolving map, once completed leading to the alluring promise of enlightenment.

But all that changed the day we found the rabbit.

The day started much like the others; with us roaming the Far-Away Forest, Mizell poking me every five minutes or so, asking if I'd heard the sound of him yet. I kept saying that I hadn't, until I suddenly did. Just ahead of us, that unpleasant scraping and creaking echoing eerily through the forest. We smiled at each other, and ran towards it laughing, abruptly falling silent when we realised what Inspector Hole-in-the-Face had brought us.

"Jesus," Mizell muttered. "What the heck is that?"

Inspector Hole-in-the-Face stood motionless, his right hand pointing directly at the mangled carcass of a white rabbit. It lay in a small pond of blood, the white fur stained with patches of crimson. I immediately gagged when I saw it, but what was worse still was the look on Mizell's face.

"Sarah," he swallowed deeply. "This is messed up. Why would you do that? That's sick!"

"It wasn't me!" I yelled hysterically. "I could never have done that! You know that Mizell!"

But the look on his face didn't change. It was disgust. Loathing. But also fear and disappointment. He slowly edged away from me, tears rolling down his face. I'd never seen him like that before, and it made me immensely sad, and incredibly angry at the same time.

"It was him!" I pointed at Inspector Hole-in-the-Face. "It was the Inspector!"

"He isn't real, Sarah!" Mizell yelled back. "You made him up! It was you all you all along! Just admit it!"

"No, it wasn't!" I sobbed. "You know me, Mizell. It wasn't me."

He just stood there blinking, like he was deciding whether or not to believe me. I got down on my knees and cradled the poor little creature in my arms, blood dripping down my clothes.

"We have to bury it," I murmured. "It's the right thing to do."

"You're right," Mizell lowered his head. "I know a place."

"Does that mean you believe me?" I looked at him and sniffed.

"It means," he met my gaze. "It means that I don't know."

Mizell sauntered toward the trail, and I followed

close behind, still holding the dead rabbit like a baby. I threw worried glances back at Inspector Hole-in-the-Face as we slowly made our way through the thick undergrowth, but he didn't seem to move at all. Still just standing there, still pointing at the spot where the rabbit had been.

"Where are we going?" I asked once we'd located the trail.

"I don't know," Mizell stopped, a worried expression on his face. "I have this feeling, like I know a place. I can't explain it."

"Freakerson!" a violent shout permeated the air. "What did I tell you?!"

We turned around to see Freddy Purcell's aggressive figure approaching us, and Mizell quickly grabbed a big rock from the side of the trail, slinking behind me stealthily.

"Fred...Freddy," I stammered, "What are you doing here? This isn't your part of the woods."

"I'm looking for my sisters bunny, Freakerson," he frowned. "What's it to you?"

He suddenly stopped dead in his tracks, eyes locked on the wretched, mangled thing in my arms. I stumbled back in fear, dragging Mizell with me, dropping the dead rabbit to the ground with trembling hands.

"I...I can explain," I muttered. "It's...it's not what it looks like."

I could practically see Freddy's eyes turning red with anger as the realisation slowly made its way to his conscious mind. He clenched both his fists, and without a warning he came running towards us screaming bloody murder.

"You'll die for this, Freakerson," he yelled. "You're just as sick as your brother was!"

I stumbled back into Mizell, and we both fell to the ground. Before I could get back up, Freddy was on top of me, locking my arms down with his knees. In his right hand he held a rock, slowly rising it above his head. In that moment I knew I was done for. I knew this is where I was going to die. But then I saw the look on Mizell's face.

He was lying on the side of the trail, eyes wide with fear. At first I thought he was scared of Freddy. Scared of me. But then he said it.

"Do you hear that?" he whispered. "What is that?"

It was the sound of metal scraping against metal, a loud, unpleasant screech, echoing through the forest. This time it was deafening. Omnipresent. Brutal and terrifying. Freddy didn't seem to care though, all his focus still targeted on me. I tried to speak. Tried to warn him. But it was too late.

A pale hand grabbed him by the throat, and he didn't even have time to scream. He was lifted into the air, and moments later I heard a sickening crunch as he was slammed into the ground with immense force. I scrambled to my feet unsteadily, only to stagger back at the sight before me.

Inspector Hole-in-the-Face was on top of the dazed Freddy, both arms raised over his horrifyingly hollow head. He turned to me slowly, the spiraling darkness of the gaping chasm ringing in my mind like a voice. If he could have, he would have smiled. Somehow I knew this. Then, with a swift movement, he turned back to Freddy, and without hesitation Inspector Hole-in-the-Face brought both fists down into his face with such force that I could see one of Freddy's eyes popping.

"Holy shit!" Mizell exclaimed, his face now pale as snow. "Holy shit, holy shit, holy shit."

Inspector Hole-in-the-Face just kept smashing both fists down into Freddy's face for minutes. Blood and other unnamable fluids squirted all over, the squelching, gruesome noises getting louder and louder, and I couldn't move an inch. I had to watch it. Had to register every one of those hits, until finally there was nothing left of his face to hit. Just a hollow crevice where there used to be a face.

Then the Inspector got to his feet, turned to Mizell and me, bowed theatrically, and disappeared into the forest once more.

"You saw him too, didn't you?" I muttered to Mizell, slumping down on the ground next to him, my head spinning, stomach churning.

"Yes," he whispered. "Yes, I saw him too."

He hugged me tightly, tears streaming down his face. He was so pale. So deathly pale. I embraced him as tightly as I could, but I was starting to feel extremely light-headed. I don't remember much else after that.

Just darkness and screeching noises and swirling black holes.

"Harold!" my mom yelled to my dad. "She's awake!"

Every bone in my body was hurting as I sat up in my bed. I was still wearing the same clothes, dirty and stained with blood. My head was still spinning, and it took me quite a while to gather my senses.

"What happened?" I muttered as my dad came into my room with a glass of water.

"You came home like this," my mom stroked my hair gently. "You didn't make any sense, crying and screaming, covered in blood and bruises. We were so worried, Sarah. So terribly worried."

I gulped down the whole glass of water in one go, and handed it back to my father.

"Inspector Hole-in-the-Face," I whispered. "He hurt him...He killed him…"

"Not another one," my father sighed. "This has to stop Sarah."

"Shut up, Harold," my mom pointed to the door. "Leave us alone."

My father sighed again, and shrugged as he left. There was this expression on his face I couldn't quite identify. Like a mixture of sadness and disappointment, but also fear and worry.

"He isn't real, Sarah," my mother said calmly.

"There is no such thing as an Inspector Hole-in-the-Face."

"He is too!" I demanded, grabbing my notebook from the nightstand, presenting to her the drawing I made of him the first time I saw him. "This is how he looks! I've seen him! You have to believe me!"

"Oh god," my mother exclaimed, a look of shock on her face as she flinched at the sight of him. "I really thought you were doing better this time."

She started crying. Long, pained, convulsive sobs. I didn't know what to do, so I just held her tight in a hug. After a while, she got up and grabbed a faded box hidden in the back of my closet. It looked vaguely familiar, but I struggled to place it in my mind.

"That's not Inspector Hole-in-the-Face," she dried her tears, and looked at me with sorrow in her eyes. She opened the box, and beckoned for me to take a look at its content. "That's your brother."

Within the box were dozens of drawings of Inspector Hole-in-the-Face, each and every one impossibly identical. "No no no no, that's not my brother," I murmured, frantically going through the drawings. "It can't be. He's dead."

My mom just stared at me, tears rolling down her face. Then she nodded softly, and turned her gaze to the door, letting out an exasperated sigh.

"We've been over this so many times, Sarah. Your brother was a troubled boy. Very troubled. It's strange you know, he was such a sweet boy once. I guess that's why we didn't see it. Refused to see it. There was a darkness in him, you see. Like a cancer of the mind, of the soul. And we should have caught it, you know? There were signs, but we just...didn't know how to interpret them."

I stared at her blankly, not knowing how to react. I remembered my brother, didn't I? I was sure of it.

"There was this one boy, Freddy Purcell. You know him, a couple of years older than you. Your brother took it out on him the most. Bullied him, called him names, but also hurt him. Broke his nose once, sprained his arm. Horrible stuff. Singled him out, tortured him daily."

My mom lowered her head. Tears dropped from her eyes down to the floor, soon forming a small pond.

"He did things to animals too. We didn't know until after, but your father found them in our backyard, slaughtered and buried. We should have known, Sarah. We should have realised sooner. Helped him. Stopped him."

She took my hand, and held it tightly in hers.

"One night your brother snuck out. He must have woken you up, you know how creaky that door used to be. You followed him. Don't know why, but you did. I guess maybe you saw it too? Maybe you wanted to help him?"

She looked at me with a slight, pained smile.

"He went out to the Purcell-farm. I guess he'd planned it for a while, because he brought the hammer with him. Broke the lock to their barn, you know, where they keep the rabbits. Freddy later told the police he woke up to the screeching sound of the barn door opening, and snuck out to check it out. What he found inside that barn, what your brother did, oh god."

"What?" I asked. "What did he do?"

"He killed them all," my mom sobbed. "Every rabbit in that barn. Smashed them over the head with the hammer, until the hammer broke. Freddy surprised him, but your brother was older, and stronger. So they fought, rolled around in that barn. Until…"

"Until what?"

"Freddy had his father's shotgun with him. It went off. Just once. One shot. That's all it took. Blew your brothers face off. Just a giant, gaping hole." She pointed to the drawings. "You must have come in soon after, dragging your doll with you. Mr. Purcell found you hugging his body, refusing to let go," She looked at me with a pained expression, eyes all red and puffy, lips quivering, "You refused to let go."

"No no no," I cried hysterically. "That's not what happened. He died in a car accident! You told me so!"

"You refused to let go, Sarah. The doctors told us you were in denial. So when you started slipping away from us, drawn into the warm comfort of your fantasy world, we decided it was best if we didn't bring it up. It was better that you stayed there for a while."

She held my face, and stared directly into my eyes. "There is no Inspector Hole-in-the-Face, Sarah. He's only in your head."

I felt nauseous and drained. It couldn't be true. It didn't make any sense. Or did it? No, no, it didn't. I was sure of it. He was real.

"Mizell saw him too!" I yelled. "He saw Inspector Hole-in-the-Face too!"

"Oh, honey," she hugged me tightly. "How many times have I told you; Mizell isn't real. He's just another imaginary friend."

I pushed her away violently, my eyes now sore from all the tears, mind overloading with pain and grief and anger. "He's not!" I yelled. "He's real! Here, look." I grabbed the photo of him from my dresser, and shoved it in her face. "Here he is! That's Mizell!"

"It's not," her lip quivered. "That's not him. That's Michael, your brother, when he was your age."

"No no no no," I tore at my hair in despair. "No no no, it can't be."

"You couldn't pronounce his name correctly, you were so young."

"No no no no," I just kept muttering.

"So you just called him Mizell."

All magical summers must come to an end. Sometimes it comes naturally; just a slow descent until the darkness engulfs you completely. Other times it's abrupt, a blink of an eye, then day becomes night. For me it was the latter.

They found Freddy's body the next day, face all smashed in with a rock. There were only two sets of prints on it; Freddy's and mine. I can't really remember much from the next couple of months, but there were a lot of questions, a lot of new faces, police, and doctors, all mixed in a haze of brief, formless moments.

They said I was mentally incompetent. That I couldn't understand what I did. I spent some time in a hospital, talked to a lot of experts who seemed very interested in what I had to say, but I can't really recall what we talked about. It's all a blur. I only remember clearly what the lead detective said. I wasn't supposed to hear it, you know. It was told off the books in whispers to parents and lawyers and faceless therapists.

"I don't think she did it," he said. "The strength required to inflict damage like that, even with a rock? It takes a grown ass man is all I'm saying."

They could never prove it of course. I don't think they even tried. But I held onto that. That was the only constant that kept me going through it all.

I'm a few years older now, and I'm doing OK. We moved shortly after everything settled. We had to. Couldn't stay there anymore. Too many bad memories. Too many dead people. I go to school, play tennis, sing in the choir, just a normal girl, you know. Nothing strange about me.

"Where are you going, honey," my mother yelled at me from the kitchen window.

"It's summer break, mom," I rolled my eyes. "I'm just going for a walk."

"OK, honey," she smiled. "Be back before dinner."

"Whatever."

I decided to follow the trail leading past the old church this morning. I always liked the look of it, so serene and peaceful.

"So, where are we headed," Mizell asked, punching me playfully in the shoulder.

"To the Echo Forest," I said. "We're gonna find him today, I'm sure of it."

"Race you to it," Mizell winked, jogging past the church.

I laughed, and chased after him.

These are beautiful times, and I'm sure you remember them yourself. There are no worries, no responsibilities, no dark thoughts; just endless days of mystery and joy, seamlessly overlapping each other.

Forever.

MY FRIEND BUG

"So, what brought you here to see me today, Peter?"

Doctor Robbins was asking a damned good question. Why was I there? Bug specifically told me not to go, yet there I was, face to face with the very thing he warned me about. Doctors. So why could I so easily disregard everything he had told me? Was it because I didn't believe him? Or was it because I believed him?

"I don't know, doc, it's kinda embarrassing you know, like on a personal level."

He gave me one of those looks only doctors can give you. You know, a combination of condescending and intrigued, like he was sort of interested, but at the same time I was totally wasting his precious time.

"Well, Peter, you're going to have to talk to me if you want my help."

There it was. I was wasting his time, yet he still wanted me to talk to him. Doctors, man. It's like Bug always told me; they don't really care about you, for them you're just another car in the garage. So if I decided to talk to him, and he found my ailment to be worthy, he'd take all the credit and add another zero to his already bursting bank account. If I didn't talk to him, and ended up dead in the gutter somewhere, he'd still have three sports cars parked outside his vast mansion. For him I was nothing but an insignificant... bug.

"Well, um, I have this friend, Bug…"

Was I really about to throw my best friend under the bus? Bug was the only one who stood by me when my life went to shit. He told me I wasn't crazy when everyone else pushed to get me committed. He let me stay in his place when my own family kicked me out. Sure, it was a shithole, but at least it wasn't the street. Bug wasn't just a friend. He was my best friend. My only friend.

"Bug?" Doctor Robbins asked snidely, "Is that a name?"

Patronizing. Not everyone was Ivy League born and bred. I just sat there in silence, staring into those soulless dollar sign eyes, not wanting to dignify the question with an answer. After a minute or two he had to blink, thus I came out victorious.

"Anyway," I said, "Bug and I invented this game, you know, to pass the time, and part of it involves this symbol we have on our arms..."

Doctor Robbins directed his gaze to my arms. I was wearing a long sleeve hoodie, so I don't really know what he expected to see.

"So, this symbol," he said, still staring at my arms, "What is it exactly? A tattoo?"

There he goes again. How it got there wasn't

important! It's all about what it means, what it stands for. I swear, if Bug hadn't held me back I would have slapped him right then and there.

"Look, I don't know if that's important," I said with a sigh, "I'm just not sure I want it anymore, you know, not sure the game is for me."

I could literally feel Bugs agitated breath on my neck. He wasn't happy. This was exactly what he had told me would happen. If you go in there, he said, they'll change you forever. But I'm not sure that's such a bad thing, all things considered. Bug was scary, and even though I loved him like my own brother, I couldn't help but to feel he was a little bit...stuck in his ways.

"So why don't you just get rid of the symbol? Quit the game?" Doctor Robbins suggested, "We don't have to let others influence our lives if we don't want them to. You are the master of your own existence, never forget that."

I scratched my neck nervously. I could hear Bug whispering in my ears. Bad things, horrible things. He wasn't happy.

"Yeah, " I said somberly, "If only it were that easy."

Doctor Robbins stroked his non-existing beard rhythmically and raised his eyebrows up and down, the crazed dance vaguely similar to a pair of drunken caterpillars. I could clearly tell he was intrigued.

"Tell me, Peter, why isn't it easy? What's holding you back?"

Bug was livid by this point. I could both hear and feel his anger, like some kind of psychosomatic explosion in the back of my mind. He was clawing around in there, burrowing deeper into my psyche, eating away at my sanity. He would do that when he wasn't happy with me. Sick little fucker.

"I made Bug a promise, you see," I murmured, "And friends don't break promises."

The pain was rising to extreme levels, and it took everything I had just to cling on to consciousness, let alone keep suffering the inane conversation with Doctor Robbins.

He leaned in closer to me,"I think this Bug character is a bad influence on you, Peter. I think we need to discuss ways we can get you away from him."

I was digging my fingernails as far as I could into my thighs, the sweet relief of the physical pain barely enough to keep me going. Tears were streaming down my face, but I couldn't help but to smile. I even think I erupted into maniacal laughter. Doctor Robbins seemed confused by my conflicting display of emotions, and I could tell he was getting anxious.

"I got you this time, Bug," I grinned, "I totally got you this time! You didn't see it coming, you little fucker!"

I removed my hood and fell to my knees convulsing with uncontrollable laughter. Doctor Robbins staggered to his feet and stared at Bug in wide-eyed shock.

"What the HELL is that thing?!" he yelled hysterically.

"It's Bug, of course!" I giggled, "What, did you think I made him up or something?"

Bug started laughing hysterically. Good one, he agreed, you really had me fooled there for a second.

"That's a fucking…" Doctor Robbins stumbled towards the door, "That's a GIGANTIC FUCKING TICK!"

I reached to the back of my neck and stroked Bug's weirdly smooth and plump body lovingly, his head of course burrowed deep into my spine. He has really grown, I thought to myself. Good for him.

Now do it, Bug echoed in my mind. You won, he is all yours now.

Doctor Robbins looked quite agitated, struggling desperately to get the door open. I guess his palms were sweaty or something, because he didn't seem to be getting anywhere. I approached him slowly, knife drawn and ready. I didn't feel anything in particular. We don't do this for the highs, or some sick perverted enjoyment or anything like that. We aren't fucking psychopaths.

"10-9," I said as I stabbed the knife forcefully into the back of Doctor Robbins' neck. He bled out in seconds, his lifeless body slowly settling on the floor, with no real pain involved at all. We're not fucking sadists either.

10-9, Bug agreed. But I'll get you next time, buddy.

I carved another X into my forearm, making it ten

X's and nine O's. We were aiming for first one to a hundred, but I guess we'd just have to see how strong our friendship really was. Traitor or T(r)ickster is a vicious and fickle game.

I looked down at the ever-growing pool of blood at my feet. I knew deep down that we wouldn't last. Either Bug would drain me dry, or I would squish him into a pulp before it got to that point. Our symbiotic relationship just wasn't sustainable, you know.

I guess that's why we came up with the game. We both knew that one of us would betray the other down the line, so we might as well get some excitement out of the arrangement. The rules were simple; we would each take a turn picking a target, and use that target to try to trick each other into thinking we wanted the other one dead. It's kinda like that card game, Bullshit, where you have to call your opponents bluffs. Except in our version someone always ended up dead. Thus far the dying part exclusively had been our targets, but one day one of us will betray the other. It is, after all, inevitable.

But until then we are just having some fun.

Good fun with my friend Bug.

FRANCINE IN THE DARK

B: Hello Francine. How are we today?

F: Fine I guess. Who are you?

B: I am Doctor Lynn, but you can call me Beverly. I'm here to ask you some very simple questions. You don't have to answer them, but it would be really, really helpful.

F: When can I go home?

B: We need to understand what happened to you first. Make sure you are safe. I understand they found you in the forest? How did you get there?

F: I got lost.

B: I see. Do your family live near the forest?

F: I think so.

B: You told the officers you couldn't show them. That

it was in the dark. Can you tell me more about the dark?

F: I don't know, I'm really not supposed to...

B: Don't worry, Francine. I just want to help you. I won't tell anyone. I'm not allowed to either, just like you.

F: Well, OK, I guess.

B: The dark. Can you explain it for me?

F: You are taken there when you are little. Everyone in my family is in the dark now. Everyone except my Pa. He says it's to keep us safe.

B: How little? How old were you when you were taken to the dark?

F: I don't know, five maybe?

B: Do you have any brothers or sisters? Are they also in the dark?

F: I have a sister, and I...I had a big brother.

B: What happened to him? Your brother?

F: He couldn't...he didn't...

B: It's OK, you don't have to…

F: He was too old, Pa said.

B: How about your mother?

F: Ma died when I was very little. I can't remember her.

B: Do you remember anything before the dark?

F: A little, not very much. It was all very shiny before Pa took out the bulbs.

B: The bulbs?

F: Yes, the seeing bulbs. Pa said he'd get better ones, ones that didn't show the ugly, and then we didn't have to be in the dark no more.

B: Oh, Francine.

F: What is it?

B: Your father can't do that. He lied to you.

F: No, Pa wouldn't lie. He can do it, you'll see.

B: He can't replace, what did you call them…the seeing bulbs.

F: What do you call them?

B: Eyes, Francine. We call them eyes.

PATCHES

"Corny" Connor Copperfield was a weird kid. We all thought so. He wore thick horn-rimmed glasses. Corny as heck. He had fiery red scruffy hair and pallid skin with more freckles than any fifth grader could count. We knew that, because one day a bunch of fifth graders held him down and started counting. They got to 442 before they had to give up. I guess that's how far fifth graders can count.

He was sort of my friend though. Well, as close to a friend someone like Corny could have I guess. Kids can be cruel like that. If one of the cooler kids has it in for you, you're basically an unwanted pariah until you hit puberty. Joel McKenna was our cool kid. He was in seventh grade and had a nose ring. Cool as heck that nose ring. He didn't like Corny one bit. Well, except for as a punching bag. He quite enjoyed him then.

Corny was tough though, I'll give him that. He rarely flinched, never cried, and definitely never tattled. He was too smart for that. I think that's what fuelled Joel's anger; Corny was just so much smarter than him. Better than him in just about every conceivable way. I guess he realised already then that Corny most likely would grow up to become something special, while he would be stuck perpetually in some dead end job. They were both wrong though, as it turned out.

There was something brewing inside that awkward pale frame of Corny. I don't think anyone but me could see it, but it was definitely there. Some kind of darkness I suppose, deep and potent; a repressed burning hatred just begging for release. You wouldn't know it by looking at him, but the constant abuse from everyone was really eating him up inside, filling the void with seething detestation. I wish I could say I was a good friend, that I stood up for him, maybe helped him in some way, but truth be told I did my best to avoid him.

You see, I wasn't his friend by choice. It was more of a geographically forced friendship than anything; he lived right across the street from me. When you, as a kid, live across the street from another kid, and you are both the same age, you are forced to be friends. That's just the rules.

At school I'd hide from him when I could. If I was seen with him it would be social suicide, and I'd be forced to join him as Joel's punching bag. I didn't want that. So I made sure to stay away from the places I knew he frequented, and surround myself with people I knew he didn't get along with. I was a shitty friend, I know, but I had my reasons. Well, I had a reason.

He was freaking weird, man. I mean, really, really weird.

The first time I realised just how weird Corny

was, we were at his house. His mom was out (she was a single mother, I'm not sure what happened to his dad), and we were playing in his room. They were pretty poor, so he didn't have a lot of toys, and I guess I sort of sat there in boredom, looking at this strange jar he had by his bed. When I shook it, I could hear a soft rustling, sort of like a maracas. I opened the lid to look at what was in it, when Corny snatched it away from me.

"Don't touch that!" he said angrily. "That's for Patches."

"Who?" I asked. He'd never mentioned that name before.

"Patches!" he said. "She's my friend."

I just shrugged and found a toy soldier to play with. After a while Corny had to go to the toilet, and the moment he left, I quickly grabbed the jar, opened it, and peered into it curiously.

I almost threw up because of the smell. The sight wasn't much prettier. It was nails and hair. Like, a jar full of fingernails, toenails, patches and strands of hair. I closed the lid and put the jar back, and got the hell out of there.

The second time I realised just how weird Corny was, we were at my house. My mom forced me to invite him over, and I reluctantly agreed after she threatened to sell my Nintendo. We were sitting in my room, sort of awkwardly trying to figure out what to do, when he suddenly had to use the toilet. I don't know, I just found it strange. He had arrived minutes earlier; surely he'd had plenty of opportunities to relieve himself before he came over.

I followed him to the toilet, and pretended to walk away. He didn't lock the door, and stayed in there for quite some time. Far too long. I pressed my ear against the door, but I couldn't hear anything. What the heck was he doing in there? I stealthily opened the door and slowly stuck my head in.

"What the hell are you doing?!" I yelled furiously.

Look, I really don't want to be too graphic here, but if I hadn't been so upset, so angry, I would've projectile vomited all over the bathroom. Corny wasn't on the toilet. He was rummaging around in the trash next to the toilet. He'd brought a small plastic bag that he was filling up with...stuff. Toenail clippings, sure. Strands of hair. My moms used tampons. My baby brothers used diapers. And not only was he stealing our waste. He was smelling it too.

And...tasting it.

Corny didn't stick around. He got this weird panicked expression, and scuttered down the stairs like a scared rat. I think our forced friendship ended that day. He knew it was over. I definitely knew it was over. I wasn't going anywhere near him again.

I wish I could say that the story ended there. But that's just the beginning I'm afraid. The context, you could say.

A few weeks after the incident a fair amount of pets started going missing in the neighborhood. Mrs. Hutchinson's cat (Snowberry? Whiteberry? Something like that), Dan the Dog's dog Danny, and a few more I can't remember. The forest was a stone's throw away, and sure, you'd expect a few to fall prey to foxes and other woodland predators, but not dozens of them the same week.

I immediately suspected Corny. I don't know why, but I guess it was the darkness I saw in him. That pure, unfiltered hate. Maybe something had snapped in him when I caught him doing...whatever he was doing. I couldn't be sure, but he had been acting weird lately. Weirder than usual. And that's some extreme levels of weird. He hadn't been to school in a few days, and when I saw him he was always either heading for, or coming back from, the forest. I told my mom about it, but she wouldn't hear of it. Connor was such a sweet and well-behaved boy she'd just say, and then threaten to sell my Playstation if I didn't stop being mean to him.

More pets went missing the following weeks, and not just in our neighborhood. People from all over town were reporting their beloved cats and dogs and hamsters and bunnies missing, and our local store window was literally overflowing with crudely written posters begging for any information.

But no one cared. Well, no one with authority cared, I should say. Probably foxes they said. Or badgers. Or eagles. Or any explanation that would keep them from actually doing something about it. I didn't have any pets, my mother had all the allergies ever invented, so I wasn't really affected, but a lot of my friends were totally devastated. So I told them who did it. Well, I told Joel. I wanted those cool credits badly.

"Corny" Connor Copperfield took the pets.

I don't think Joel really cared about the animals. He just wanted a reason to kick the shit out of Corny. Any old excuse would do, but stealing and (possibly) killing pets? That wasn't just an excuse. That was a call for justice. And justice would be served.

There was a bunch of us present, and we were all questioned by the police a few days later. We gathered at the start of the forest trail, watching as Joel, adjusting his cool-as-heck nose ring nonchalantly, wandered into the forest after the badly injured Corny. Joel had beaten the shit out of him, and more than likely broken his ankle and his left arm. Both his eyes were blue and swollen shut, his glasses were shattered, and he was bleeding profusely from a deep cut on his scalp. He limped into the forest like a wounded animal with Joel in close pursuit.

Look, I didn't enjoy it. In fact, I hated it. I know it was a shitty thing to do. Sure, I was mad at Corny for what he had done, but he didn't deserve this. He didn't deserve to be chased into the forest like some freak outcast.

That's the last we ever saw of Corny. And Joel. Well, sort of.

The police didn't know what the hell had happened. Big surprise, bunch of talentless, lazy hacks the lot of them. They searched the forest front to back several times over, and teamed up with the volunteers they kept it going for weeks. But there was nothing. No trace. No nothing. It was like they had vanished into thin air.

The weirdest part, according to Sarah, the sheriff's daughter, was the dogs. The canine unit. They couldn't get them into the forest. They were too afraid. Even if they dragged them in there, they would do nothing except lie down and whimper. Something in that forest freaked them out, Sarah said, and her father didn't want to look into it. He was scared too, she said. Deathly afraid of what might be out there.

Corny's mom moved soon after. I guess she couldn't stand the place anymore. Can't say I blame her; I for one will never return. Not after what I saw.

Not after I saw Patches.

It was a few years after the event. Sarah and I (yes, we became a thing, much to her father's dismay, lol, useless bastard) were walking her dog on the forest trail when it suddenly started acting strange. It sort of panicked, dragging Sarah away from the trees, whimpering like crazy. Sarah thought maybe it had stepped on something, but I could clearly see movement in the bushes further in. I told Sarah to stay back, as I went in to investigate.

I could smell it before I could see it. I don't really like the term indescribable, but that's exactly what it was. I can't find the words to accurately describe the rank odour that attacked my nasal cavities. Death? Decomposition? A conglomeration of all smells vile and detestable?

I had to stop and cover my nose, but couldn't help but to wretch and cough. I guess it must have heard me, because the bushes suddenly stopped moving. I started edging closer, trying to stay as silent as I could. When I was maybe a few feet away from the bush, I accidentally stepped on a dry twig, and in an instant Patches came out of hiding.

It was big. About the size of a large dog. If the smell was indescribable, its appearance was too describable. I'm not sure what it was. Or how it came to be. But I think I know where it all started.

With that jar.

I guess you could call it a mouth. A yawning chasm encircled by sharp toenail clippings and patches of thin, frizzy hair. It was centered on a bulging, amorphous mass, patched together by putrid, decomposing fragments of animal and human waste alike. Faeces, blood, nails, strands of hair, patches of skin, snouts, paws, tails, all conjoined to form the abhorrent abomination before me. It moved by shifting its foul, disgusting internal liquids, adjusting its center of balance, and quite elegantly so.

We sort of just stood there silently staring at each other. I don't even know if it had eyes, but it sure looked like it knew exactly where I was. I can never be certain about this, but I think I would've died that day if it wasn't for Sarah. Thankfully she ignored my warnings, and came looking for me, dragging the dog along with her. I guess Patches sensed it was outnumbered, and slowly started retreating back into the bush. That's when I saw it. Something I'd recognize anywhere.

A very cool looking nose ring.

It was still attached to Joel's nose, buried within a mass of shit and diapers and tampons. It was almost poetic. Patches slithered, or crawled, or rolled, into the bush, and sped out the other side with some haste. A thought occurred to me then. Corny. Was he still alive, roaming out there in the wilderness with his beloved pet, finally accepting his role as an outcast, a pariah?

I got my answer moments later.

It was the last I saw of Patches. I never went looking for it. Who the fuck in their right mind would? But just before it disappeared into the gloomy shadows of the forest, I spotted something. Covered by strands of hair and crooked toenail clippings. A patch of human skin.

With more freckles than any fifth grader could count.

DEAR MOM

I can never forget that night. Not a single moment of it. I still wake up hearing that horrid scream. I can still picture that steadily growing pool of crimson slowly inching its way under the bedroom door. I can still imagine you clearly, face frozen in shock and horror, your bloodsoaked body perfectly still on the hardwood floor. And to think, mere hours before everything was peaceful. None of us knew. Knew what opening that book would lead to.

It was Brie who found it. We were just playing around in the attic when she accidently kicked loose that floorboard. Father had always told us to stay away from there. It was too dangerous. We could fall through the floor. Break our necks. For a moment I thought that's exactly what happened; that Brie stepped through the brittle wood, her neck snapping as she hit the floor all the way down there. But it was just a loose floorboard.

"You alright, Brie?" I said. You always told me she'd need a kind and protective big sister, so I tried my best to be one. It was hard at times, you know how she can be, but I think you'd be proud of us if you could see us now.

"Yeah," Brie mumbled. "But come take a look at this. I think I found a secret."

I carefully made my way towards her, making sure to watch my step. She was in a corner, squatting over the hole left by the missing floorboard. She reached into it with both hands and gently lifted the cursed thing out of it. I remember thinking how ancient it looked. It was torn and ragged, every page smudged and stained, like it had been passed down countless generations.

"What is it?" I asked.

"It's a book, silly." Brie said rolling her eyes.

"I know that," I said. "But what's it about?"

Brie was only eight, so she couldn't really read all that well yet. She flipped through the pages, mouthing the easy words when she found them. BLOOD. PAIN. After a while she just shrugged, and handed me the book instead.

"I don't know," she said. "But it has all these strange pictures and words in it."

The cover didn't reveal anything about its content. It was faded and grey, fairly dull and anonymous, rough to the touch. But the moment I started reading the first page I knew we had found something we weren't supposed to. Something dark and secret. Something that shouldn't be. Something we were far too young to understand.

But we couldn't help ourselves. We were just kids. Curious, stupid kids.

I find myself wondering what would have happened if we'd never found the book. How would our lives have gone then? What if we had kept it a secret, Brie and me? Would someone else have stumbled upon it years later? How would reading the book have changed them? How would it have changed us? I know it doesn't matter; that I'm just tormenting myself, but I don't think it's possible to move on without at least considering the what ifs.

I've been asked to describe the content of the book more times than I can count. I could never do it. Not really. I can remember minor details, like the ungodly pictures, or random sentences that my ten year old mind could comprehend, but I could never force myself to revisit the perversity of it as a whole. I know deep down that I can do it. I just choose not to. I believe that my ability to do this; to bury the true meaning and existence of it deep down in my subconscious, is the only thing keeping me from going insane.

And I have to hold it together. That was my promise to you. Hold it together for Brie.

We sat there studying the book for hours. I read most of it aloud so Brie could understand, but I don't think either of us truly got the meaning behind the words. Most of it was in plain english, describing heinous rituals and acts so defiled and corrupted that I had to take pauses to allow the tainted words to ease their way into my mind. Then came the pictures. Horrible, gut-wrenching images, some of which I couldn't even stand to look at for more than a second.

Every chapter had a name. I remember that vividly. Some were strange, foreign, unknown, others I could recognize. Lilith. Her portrait is still imprinted in my mind. Whenever I close my eyes, I can see her clear as day. Wretched, twisted, horrible. She wasn't the worst, but she was the one we looked at the longest.

That's when you came, mom.

We didn't hear you. We were mesmerized by that foul book. Entranced by the blasphemous morbidity of it. So when you snatched the thing right out of my fingers I couldn't help but to scream. I didn't mean to. I think you understood that.

"Mom!" I yelled. "Why did you do that?"

You gave me a stern I'm the grown up here-look and grabbed Brie by the arm. "Didn't your dad tell you two to stay out of here?" You said. I remember I shrugged and reached for the book. You yanked it away and pointed to the stairs.

"Dinner. Now. Daddy's running late, so we'll just have to eat without him today."

We gathered around the dinner table. You placed the book on the kitchen counter. Didn't even look at it. I was kinda worried. I don't know why, but it felt like we'd done something bad. And I don't mean sneaking up to the attic-bad. Something really bad.

We didn't say much. Talked about school and such. Idle talk. But then, as we were cleaning the table, your eyes fell on the book. And you opened it. The way your face changed. That's what I always come back to. That moment of shock. Your plate fell from your hands, shattered into tiny pieces on the floor. But that look. That expression.

"Wh-where did you find this?" you asked as you flipped the page with trembling fingers.

I couldn't speak. I'd never seen you like that before. I'd seen you upset, angry, disappointed, sad, scared, but not all of them at once. You were pale. Like all the blood had drained from your face.

"Where did you find this?!" you turned to us and yelled, tears now streaming down your face.

"In-In-In the attic," I muttered. "It was hidden. Brie tripped over a loose board and found it."

"I didn't mean to," Brie sobbed. "It was an accident."

You stood there, wide-eyed, trembling, crying, just staring at us for what felt like minutes. I don't know what went through your head, mom, but I'm sorry. Sorry for everything that happened. You didn't deserve any of it.

"Did you girls read it," you whispered. "Did you look at it."

I shook my head and kept staring at the floor. I didn't like lying to you, but I knew we were in trouble. That we'd done something bad. But I just couldn't understand what. Brie cried, poor little thing. She thought you hated us for it.

"It's OK," you said. "It's OK. It's gonna be OK."

You calmed down somehow. I don't know how you did it. I could never have done it. It was like you swallowed the storm, devoured it, buried it deep down.

You knew what was coming next, didn't you? I think you realised at that moment what would happen that night. But you couldn't tell us.

You told us to go to our rooms. Play safe for a while. Until bedtime. We listened. Didn't want to upset you again. But I snuck down. I just wanted to check on you. I saw you sitting there, crying, too repulsed to look at the book, yet still your eyes were drawn to it. Did you consider calling someone? I've always wondered that. Why did you feel like taking this on all by yourself? I guess I'll never know.

Brie fell asleep in my bed. I drifted off soon after. Held her tight like a stuffed animal. Before that night I didn't understand why you wanted me to protect her. She could learn on her own, like I did. She didn't need me. I understand now though. There are some things, horrible, unspeakable things, that you never wanted her to see. To experience. To understand.

I can never forget that night. Not a single moment of it. I woke up hearing that horrid scream coming from your bedroom. As I approached it I saw the growing pool of crimson slowly inching its way under the door. With a gentle push it swung open, revealing you, face frozen in shock and horror, your bloodsoaked body perfectly still on the hardwood floor.

My father's corpse was a mangled mess. I don't know how many times you stabbed him, but there was a gaping hole where his stomach should be. There was so much blood. Everywhere. I couldn't move. Just stood there trembling like a leaf.

"I'm sorry, Natalie," you muttered. "I'm so sorry."

They couldn't identify all of them. The girls in my father's perverse, depraved journal. A few of them were reported missing, others were assumed runaways, but many, too many, were never identified. Over twenty total. Twenty girls raped, tortured and murdered by my father, little more than footnotes in his fucking deranged, sickening manifesto.

I think you died that night, mom. Something inside you just stopped working. I could see it in your eyes. The life that was once there didn't shine through like it used to. And every time I visited you the light had faded just a tiny bit more. Until it was all gone. And then you left us. I don't blame you. I never will.

Dear mom. I'm sorry. I'm so sorry. But you saved us. We always made sure to remind you of that, Brie and me. We will never forget what you did for us. Thank you. Thank you so much.

Rest in Peace,
Love Natalie

DIGGING UP MY DAD

It's been almost 226 days since we buried my dad. That's roughly 325,000 minutes, or 19,500,000 seconds. It's not like I'm counting or anything, but it seems important somehow. To remember.

My mom says we have to move him, or else they might find him. And we don't want that, she says. Might mean a world of trouble if they do.

I'm not sure how deep he is, but it isn't six feet. More like four? Still, it isn't easy, there's a lot of dirt, and we are all so tired, my sister, my mom, and me. But it has to be done, it just can't be helped. I don't want to go to prison. I don't want any of us to go to prison.

He had it coming. That's what she said. He was a bad man, a very bad man. He shouldn't have done the things he did. He shouldn't have hurt us. And he had to pay for it. We all do, when we do bad things. That's how we learn. He wouldn't learn, though, so he had to go in the ground.

My mom backed the truck up real close to the hole. We don't need the box, she says. Just dad. Just the body.

We'd already prepared a new hole for him. A new box.

Mom helped me get him out of the box and onto the back of the truck, while my sister started shovelling the dirt back into the hole. He smelled real bad. Horrible. I almost had to puke several times. But we did it.

The new hole was miles away. It was deeper than the other one. Six feet or more. He would be safe there. No one could find him. He would serve his punishment.

He was wheezing, begging, tugging at me, but he was too weak to do anything. We replaced the I.V. bags and attached the new oxygen canisters to the box, and gently lowered him in there.

"Two years left," my mom said.

Then we buried my dad again.

THE DAY I TRIED TO LIVE

8:00 AM - Mailman

I woke the same as any other day, except a voice was in my head. I've had voices in my head for as long as I could remember, but this one was different somehow. More corporeal. Cheerier? I turned to face it, realising mid-turn what an utterly ridiculous notion that was. How could I possibly expect to address something that wasn't even there? Imagine then my surprise when the owner of the voice turned out to be none other than someone not in my head?

"Seize the day," he said. "Pull the trigger, drop the blade. And watch the rolling heads."

I couldn't immediately recognize him. Tall, blonde guy. Mid-twenties maybe? Immaculate white hoodie, piercing emerald eyes. His perfect teeth sparkled gloriously like he was in a toothpaste commercial or something.

"What's that?" I mumbled sleepily, knocking over several empty bottles as I stumbled out of bed. My hangover was still present. It had been there for months now. Drinking heavily obviously wasn't the solution.

"You gotta get up and at'em, Chris," he said cheerily. "You're coming with me today. That ought to cheer you up."

He winked, and sauntered out of my bedroom gracefully. I followed him diligently, my unbalanced exit not nearly as elegant. I think we made it all the way to the front door before I started questioning what was going on.

"Hey, wait a minute," I said confusedly. "Who the hell are you?"

He turned on his heel, his long blond hair doing that thing you'll see in shampoo commercials. "You know who I am, Chris, don't be daft, " he grinned. "You've been calling me for months now."

"What?" I asked. "Wait, who?"

"Come along now, Christopher. We'll have time for one syllable questions later," he said, disappearing out the door.

I guess I just stood for a minute trying to reboot my consciousness. To be fair to my brain, I hadn't really been giving it the best working conditions these past few months, so it wasn't solely to blame for the slow reset. After getting it back online, and reassuring it that yes, this was all very surreal, I followed the man outside.

"There we are, Chris," he said, beckoning me to join him as he paced down the street. "We'll have lots of fun today, believe me. Might even make you reconsider your choices."

We slowly walked past mrs. Cameron's property just as the mailman pulled in. I never really liked him. Short, stubby guy, with a monstrous mustache. He never seemed to smile either. I guess that's the first thing that threw me off. The unnervingly wide grin manifesting on his grubby face as he noticed us.

"Mr. S, good to see ya," the mailman said, raising his hand in greeting.

"Cornell," the man tipped an imaginary hat, and bowed gracefully. "Up to no good, I hope?"

"You know it, mr. S," he chuckled, and shuffled up the stairs toward mrs. Cameron's house.

"You know my mailman?" I asked dumbfoundedly.

"Chris, Chris, Chris," he gave me a pat on the back. "I know you all. You all come to me in time of need, and you are all so very, very needy."

I stared at the mailman as he hopped up to mrs. Cameron's front door. I couldn't put my finger on it, but something seemed different about him. Something felt really, really off. As it turns out, I was only half-right. It was something really, really out.

"Is he?" I mumbled. "Is that?"

"His innards? Guts? Intestines? Yes, quite the astute observation, Christopher," mr. S said.

It wasn't very hard to see now that I was aware of them. Flopping around disgustingly as his stubby persona struggled with the steps. The wound in his abdomen was exposed, a perfectly cut vertical slit from his chest down to his groin. If I wasn't already sick to my stomach from the hangover, I would've doubled over and vomited what little content I had left from the night before.

"You see things as they are now, Chris," mr. S said, grinning widely. "You're finally living."

"I...I don't understand," I said, gawping at the horrible sight of it.

"Cornell here isn't a good man," he said, waving his finger from side to side. "In fact, I've yet to meet a good man. Or woman. You all have these yawning chasms of wonderful diabolical potential. Design flaw I suppose. Any which way, he decided that gutting his mother for the inheritance was a good way of tapping into that potential. I was there to help him pin it on his brother. Rather dreary deal, I must confess, but it all wrapped up rather nicely."

"So he got away with it?" I asked, still struggling to take my eyes off the dancing guts spraying blood everywhere.

"No one truly gets away with it, Christopher," he laughed heartily. "They all get what's coming to them in the end."

We started walking again when mrs. Cameron answered the door. Such a sweet old lady, mrs. Cameron. Brought me dinner for a week after Amber died. Even came to the funeral. I think she was the only one of my neighbors who attended. The rest of them couldn't even look me in the fucking eyes.

"Are you the devil?" I suddenly asked. I suppose I needed to know just who I was dealing with.

"Are you the human?" he chuckled. "It's a pointless concept, Chris. Let it go. Enjoy life now that you're truly living it."

He sat down on the bench by the bus stop, whistling a discordant tune. I joined him, and shuffled awkwardly back and forth as he kept changing positions. I suppose we must have been sitting there for quite a while doing nothing when mr. Shepherd popped out from his house across the street. I let out a surprised yelp at the sight of him.

9:00 AM - Like Suicide

"Such a beautiful sight, isn't he?" mr. S sang. "Just like suicide."

"What...what," I murmured silently.

Mr. Shepherd was naked, bloated and blue, his head angled like the neck was broken or something. For some reason I grabbed onto the bench, feeling the rough wood digging into my palms. The sweet relief of pain calmed me some.

"Hung himself," mr. S said. "Had second thoughts just before he crossed over. Couldn't live with what he'd done, but couldn't face the other side either. We get a lot of those."

"What...What did he do?" I asked, a single tear escaping my eye.

"Oh boy, extensive rap sheet on that one," he chuckled. "Started with cats, ended with his niece. Don't worry, though, Christopher. I set up a doozy of a deal for him. He'll face the fire, have no fear. Long time coming."

The bloated corpse abomination of mr. Shepherd caught sight of us, and quickly wobbled back inside again. I spotted his pale blue, dead eyes in the window soon after, peering out at us from behind bile-green curtains.

"They can't all handle it," he patted me on the back, and stood up. "Come along, Christopher. We've only just getting started. Such a wonderful day, isn't it?"

I glanced up to look at the sun, but it was nowhere to be found. Beneath the black the sky looked dead. I felt a harrowing cold chill enter every cell of my body as we slowly paced down the bloodstained street. Tar-black shadows and screams enveloped us in a cacophony of horror, and for a fleeting moment I remembered how it felt like to be alive.

10:00 AM - Limo Wreck

"Ah, this one should interest you," mr. S said, pointing at the burning car wreck that used to be mr. Artis' house. I didn't even flinch at the absurdity anymore. There was just too much of it. I guess I'd just conformed to the idea that I wasn't in control anymore. "Remind you of anything?" he looked at me, and laughed.

It didn't, but it also did. I looked down at my feet, realising I was still in my raggedy old pyjamas, and felt an instant surge of anger rising. I was able to ignore it somehow. I suppose I knew nothing good would come of it.

"Yes," I just said, still staring at my bare feet.

Mr. Artis sat in the driver's seat, his charred black body convulsing gruesomely. As the flesh slowly melted away, I could see his bluish veins throbbing steadily underneath. I wouldn't have recognized him if it weren't for the tattoo. He did it himself, you know. The tattoo. Artis the Artist, he'd call himself. It was a fine one, to be sure. A pontiac firebird.

"Mr. Artis here left a young mother and her child to burn to death after a particularly heinous car accident," he said, peering into the window of the burning car. A white limo. You don't see limos anymore. A thing of the past. Just like me. "He's been trying to reach me. Wants me to take the pain away. Still ironing out the details."

"What's the point to all of this?" I suddenly blurted out in frustration.

"We're getting to that, Christopher," he chuckled. "Let's cut through the park, shall we? Maybe a tint of green will help you calm down."

We left the screaming mr. Artis behind, and crossed the street. We waded through the blood and filth and fire, but it all felt perfectly natural now. Like it had always been there.

11:00 AM - Let Me Drown

I've never really enjoyed the outside very much. No ceiling, no barriers, nothing holding you back. The park was nice though. Tall trees, fresh grass, a lovely little playground. Amber always wanted kids. I was kind of on the fence about them, but she would have convinced me down the line. That's just who she was. That's just how much I loved her.

"There she is," mr. S beamed, looking into the swirling black maelstrom of the sandpit. I peered over his shoulder cautiously, catching a brief glimpse of the tortured visage of mrs. Yamamoto down there before pulling back quickly. Tiny black fingers covered her, crawled over her, reaching all the way down her throat. There had to be thousands of them. Millions.

"Let me drown," mrs. Yamamoto gargled hideously. "Let me drown."

"Lovely," mr. S said, grinning widely. "You see, Christopher? She's in pain, just like you. Just like you she's not to fault for her torment. Innocent. Pure. Still she calls on me, me, to bring back her son. Perished in a pool years ago, little Hiro. Water in his lungs, I guess."

"Will you?" I asked, edging away from the sandpit nervously. "Will you bring him back?"

"Half of him, perhaps," he chuckled. "There's a science to these things, Christopher. That's what I'm trying to show you."

We continued through the park, and I stopped

briefly to smell the severed eye flowers. The stench of them reminded me of home, of sweet moments, and carefree boredom, and the bliss of not knowing. Oh, how I longed back to the Superunknown. Fresh tendrils crept up my nose as I plucked one of the disfigured ones, snorting the iris seeds right into my brain.

Mrs. Yamamoto kept drowning in the distance, swallowed by guilt she didn't need, and hope she didn't want. Mr. S threw his head back and laughed heartily when I told him.

Told him that I felt alive.

12:00 - She Likes Surprises

We followed the flesh brick road all the way back to my street. The squelching noises beneath my bare feet didn't bother me as much anymore. The lukewarm blood filling the cracks between my toes felt strangely soothing, and I was starting to enjoy the constant smell of rot and decay too.

"We'll sneak in here," mr. S said, pointing at mrs. Everman's house. "She likes surprises."

I'm pretty sure her house wasn't normally painted in the color of millions of squirming maggots, but I could be mistaken. After all, reality is what we make of it, isn't it? A slight trauma to the head can change everything, you know. Then all of a sudden up is face, and red is left, and maggots are paint.

"Shhhh," mr. S gestured for me to stay quiet. "We don't want to wake her."

We silently snuck through the house, finding mrs. Everman asleep atop a pile of decomposing corpses in the living room. Mr. S kept pointing to the corpses, rolling his emerald eyes at me when I shrugged back at him. I was having a hard time keeping the hungry maggots from crawling all over me though, so I felt like he could cut me some slack.

"What?" I whispered. "What is it?"

Mr. S pointed to the corpses again, and this time it finally dawned on me what was so special about them. They were all the same corpse. Beautiful carcasses they were, a lovely young woman, now greenish and bloated and gaseous and maggot-ridden, but still gorgeous.

"Her daughter," mr. S whispered. "She disowned her ten years ago. Died a million deaths, the pretty young thing, before she finally ended it all in a filthy motel room. Such a waste, don't you think?"

Mr. S paced back and forth between the vast pile of the same corpse and me, whistling cheerily.

"Wakey wakey!" he suddenly yelled at the top of his lungs. Mrs. Everman awoke with a harrowing shriek, and then found herself slowly sinking into the rotting mound of her daughter's corpses. I could see the fear in her eyes, the absolute horror of what she was facing, but I couldn't feel anything.

Mr. S doubled over with laughter while I just stood there blinking the maggots out of my eyes.

"If this doesn't make you feel," he finally said, drying his tears. "It doesn't mean you've died."

1:00 PM - Spoonman

We left Mrs. Everman clawing and chewing her way through the corpse mountain, and sauntered down to old mr. Sundquist's quaint little house. I'd always adored his cozy little cottage thing, but I don't think I'll ever see it the same way again. It resembled a monstrous pile of oozing garbage, like a rotting landfill, vile, foul-smelling liquid seeping down from it. We slipped in under a torn plastic tarp, finding the naked body of mr. Sundquist lying in a pool of disgusting sludge.

"Hey, Spoonman," mr. S said, slapping the lethargic, hollow-cheeked face of mr. Sundquist aggressively. "Time for a refill."

Mr. Sundquist sat up mechanically, producing fleshly spoons instead of fingers on his hands. Mr. S filled the wrinkly spoon-limbs with a brown liquid he magicked out of thin air, before setting the whole puddle of sludge on fire with a simple snap of his fingers. We stood silently watching the old man burn, every once in a while stabbing himself with a spoon, sighing deeply as the liquid spread through his system in the shape of black pulsating veins.

"Addicts are the easiest," Mr. S remarked. "No fun, really. They'll gladly sell their own spouse for another fix. Interestingly enough, that's exactly what our Spoonman here did. Peddled his own wife off like she was an object. Strange old breed, you lot. You seem to have an innate penchant for self-inflicted damnation."

He turned to me, smiling slyly. His piercing gaze met my tired eyes, and a nod of approval followed. "Not you though, Christopher," he said. "You're different, aren't you?"

"I am?" I asked.

"Head down, hide that smile," he grinned. "Still a few to go."

2:00 PM - 4th of July

Mr. S whistled the same discordant tune over and over again as we continued down the street. There were only a couple of houses left, but for some reason I didn't want it to end. I looked up at the Black Hole Sun slowly eating away at the tumorous world, and I felt a violent peace overcome me.

"Let's check in on mr. Kim real quick," mr. S said. "He's what they call a real character."

Mr. Kim was a gentle old man. Korean immigrant. The kind of person you'd swear could never even hurt a fly. Amber loved to engage with him in small talk. Real interesting guy, she'd tell me. We found him sitting on his front porch, rocking back and forth on a chair made from the body of his wife. She was still alive, her weird corpse stretched and angled and broken. I could see one of her eyes blinking at me, centered on the back of the chair, in between folds of wrinkly, hairy patches of skin.

"Mr. Kim loves this country, you know," mr. S said, running his hands down the warty, leathery surface of the sickening chair. "That's why they call him the King of the 4th around here. He's also a 4th generation wifebeater. Funny how numbers work, isn't it? You put so much value in them, but in the end they don't care about you at all."

I could see now that there was no way to tell where mr. Kim started and mrs. Kim ended. They were fused together in a perpetual fleshly embrace, the disfigured, warped mouth of mrs. Kim slowly devouring the back of mr. Kim's neck. The blood poured from the wound, down into her mouth, and back into mr. Kim. I caught myself smiling at the beautiful parasitic bond. Quite romantic when you think about it.

"Head high, Christopher," mr. S chuckled. "You've got to smile."

When we left mr. Kim's porch, a loud high-pitched shriek echoed as the black sky erupted in crimson colors. Happy 4th of July, I thought, as I sampled drops of the blood rain pouring down on us.

3:00 PM - My Wave

Ben Thayil was my next door neighbor, and our very last visit. I'd considered him a friend before Amber died, but I hadn't seen much of him since the funeral, which he didn't even attend. We walked past his bike, a black and red custom Harley, and stopped briefly to enjoy the artwork on his surfboards, of which he had mounted on his garage. They were all different depictions of Amber engaged in various sexual acts with him.

"I must say," mr. S stroked his chin thoughtfully,

"I'm not usually one for vulgar shock value pieces, but these would fit quite nicely over my fireplace."

I suppose I always knew, deep down. I chose to ignore it, to swallow my pride. I put Amber on a pedestal, and refused to acknowledge the ugliness, the flaws, the wrinkles and rot inside her. I still did. Even when staring it right in the face, I chose to ignore it. I did swing a leg out, however, accidently connecting with the bike's kickstand, sending it crashing into the jagged bone surface of the driveway with a loud metallic bang.

"Let's go say hi to the old chap, what do you say?" mr. S grinned.

Mr. S set fire to the garage with a snap of his fingers, and we slipped inside Ben's front door, finding him sobbing inconsolably in his bedroom.

"You stole it," he murmured in between pathetic whimpers. "My wave. You stole my wave."

He was old, but not in age or numbers, or even in appearance. It was like he'd aged out of his own existence, like he no longer had any concept of who he was. He crawled around on the floor, licking his own tears, wailing hysterically.

"Early onset dementia," mr. S shook his head solemnly. "All those wonderful memories of backstabbing you slowly fading from him. Soon he won't remember a single thing. Just a blank mind, a consciousness lost inside an empty echo. Pretty cool, eh?"

I gave him a weak nod, and sat down beside the pathetic shadow of Ben, patting him on his head idly. I still didn't feel anything for him. But I felt something for me. I felt alive.

"I suppose this marks the end to our little walk-about," mr. S said, strolling out of the bedroom. "We've only got one house left."

4:00 PM - Fell On Black Days

Sauntering back into my own mess of a house, I couldn't help but to feel a weird sense of relief. It was like a burden had been removed from my shoulders, a veil lifted from my eyes, a fog fading from my mind. Clarity, I suppose you could call it. Life would be another word for it.

"You fell on Black Days, Christopher," mr. S said, as we sat down on my couch. "But unlike the others you don't demand. You don't need. Why is that, you think?"

"What good will it do?" I asked. "It won't change anything. I'll still be hollow."

Mr. S threw his head back and laughed. "Is that so?" he grinned. "So you're telling me there's nothing you want? Nothing that will make it better?"

With a lightning fast move he stuck his hand into my chest, all the while holding my gaze with those imposing emerald eyes. I convulsed in unimaginable pain as he rummaged around in there, his icy cold fingers digging into every crevice, breaking bones, pushing muscles and tissue aside, clawing at nerve endings. After what felt like ages of relentless torment, he pulled his arm out, holding my beating, shrivelled heart in his hand.

"It's this thing, isn't it?" he held it out and stared at it. "The symbolic organ of love. It's just muscles and tissue, Christopher. A glorified blood pump. I could put a piggy's ticker in you right now, and you'd feel no different."

I coughed up blood, gasping for air, convulsing uncontrollably as I collapsed on the floor.

He shrugged, and smiled. "Can't argue with that, I suppose," he chuckled. "Here you go, Chris. I guess you need this thing more than I do."

He pushed the heart right back into the gaping hole in my chest, and I could suddenly breathe again. There was no blood, no wound, no scar. I scrambled up from the floor, edging away from him nervously.

"I know you want it, Christopher," he stood up from the couch, his lanky frame suddenly twice my size. "I could hear you calling me. There is one thing you want more than anything else."

I swallowed deeply, and nodded, my gaze lowering to the floor. "I want to know who did it," I said. "I want the person who did it to feel my pain."

A horrible laughter echoed through the house as mr. S approached me. "There we have it, young Christopher," he said darkly. "Finally we're being honest with each other."

Amber died in a hit and run, just a couple miles down the road. They never found the bastard, but they assumed it was a drunk driver because of all the erratic skid marks at the scene. She could have made it, someone once told me. Just had to notify the paramedics. That's all. A simple anonymous phone call was all it would have taken. Instead she died cold and alone, her mangled body hidden in a filthy, dark ditch for hours.

"I'll make it happen," mr. S said, holding out his right hand. "I can make them pay."

Tears filled my eyes as I shook his hand. A morbid sensation lingered for hours after the handshake, like I'd unleashed something blasphemous and unholy. That's exactly what I'd done, of course, and I was painfully aware of that. But I didn't care. I still felt more alive in that moment than I had for years.

"Mr. S?" I said as we'd finalized our deal. "What happens next?"

"Call me Sam," he grinned. "We're friends now after all. Just keep living, Chris, and it'll all work out. You can trust me. I never lie."

I knew I'd see him again at some point. And I did, years later, but that's another story entirely. I felt this immense sadness as he departed, his cheery figure disappearing in a macabre fountain of blood and gore, leaving me alone in the gloomy dusk of my own somber tomb. I sighed, and smiled, and collapsed on my couch.

I moved out the very next day. Packed my shit and hit the road. There was nothing for me there anymore, and with my newfound knowledge of the neighborhood's dark occupants, I felt it best to move on.

I learned a few weeks later that mrs. Cameron had

passed away. She died horribly in a car accident, her mangled old body thrown to the side of the road in a hit and run. Apparently she'd been conscious for days, paralyzed by the impact, as wild animals slowly picked her broken, twisted frame apart. She must have been in so much pain, they told me. Unimaginable torture.

I never felt alive again after that. I guess I left something behind after all?

But I will always remember the day I tried to live. I wallowed in the blood and mud with all the other pigs, and I learned that I was a liar. Just one more time around, and I might do it. Just one more time around, and I might make it.

One more time around.

MOMMY, WHY IS MY FACE INSIDE-OUT?

"**M**ommy, why is my face inside-out?"

It's a question you don't quite know how to answer, but as a parent should always expect. Kids aren't stupid. They're quite perceptive in fact. And they always tell the truth. They always ask the truth.

Molly was six when she asked me the question. A lovely little angel she was, fair-haired, blue eyed, and sweet. You couldn't help but to fall in love with her precious pure-hearted soul. We were skipping down the trail to the beat of the drums, when she suddenly stopped dead in her tracks. She just stood there in silence, eyes fixated on her feet, before asking;

"Mommy, why is my face inside-out?"

There's no easy way to answer the question of course. You could go into full professor-mode and explain to her the delicate intricacies of subcutaneous tissue, and how it pertains in regards to the details of her condition. Or you could get all philosophical and suggest to her that it's all intrinsically linked to the duality of mankind, the transitioning forces of life itself, and the alpha omega of all things.

But you know it won't satisfy her curiosity.

So instead you could look into the religious doctrines. Tell her about the dark apostate and the great conflagration. Tell her the truth of the word, and trust that she will embrace it as her own. Tell her how a face is just a lie; an instrument of the schismatic opposer, a thousand untruths woven into a single expression. Pray that she will accept this, thus readying herself for the trials down the road.

But you know it will take more than a story.

So just tell her. The brutal truth. The violent facts. Tell her why she's different, and don't hold back. Don't skimp on the grisly details. She can take it. Kids are strong, resilient, capable of overcoming great trauma. It's better to prepare them for what's coming. Better that they know early on.

"Oh, my darling Molly," I said, caressing her beautiful blonde hair. "It won't be inside-out forever."

Expect a smile of relief, but quickly move on. Don't let the frail hope linger for too long.

So you tell her in great detail about the medical procedure. How that when she comes of age they will cut deep into the skin around her face, pull off the mask, and turn it the other way around. Tell her that she has to be awake for it, to feel the blood pouring down her neck, to feel the scalpel carving into flesh, but that it will all be worth it. Because, in the end, she won't be alone. She'll be like the rest of us.

Shielded forever from the thousand untruths.

She will swallow deeply, and fall deathly silent, but she'll come to accept it. Take her hand. Skip down the trail. Join the ceremony. We are all one here. We are all the same.

As is our way.

One truth.

One face.

THE DINNER RITUAL

I'd been dating Jason Myers for two months when he finally invited me to meet his parents. He'd been strangely reluctant to the idea, having met my parents on multiple occasions already, and I was really starting to get anxious about the whole thing. Was he embarrassed? Was I not good enough for his parents? But when he finally called and asked if I wanted to join him for dinner at his parents house, I was over the moon. It meant that he took us seriously.

I knew that his family had rather eclectic beliefs, some pagan mix of something or other, but Jason had always seemed like the poster boy for normality. Well, almost. He told me he didn't really practise the religion, but that he had deep respect for his parents who did, and he warned me before meeting them that they might be a bit...different.

I didn't mind different though. Most of the time I even welcomed it.

I showed up a bit early, having left with more than enough time to locate the address. I wasn't very familiar in that part of town, and all the houses more or less looked identical to me.

"Look for the Stone" Jason said, which didn't make much sense until it suddenly did. I'd driven through the narrow streets several times, glancing left and right for any clues, when suddenly I saw it.

It was massive. A dusky obelisk carved from what looked like obsidian. What a bizarre freaking garden ornament was all that I could think.

I pulled up in the driveway, got out, and just stood there looking at the stone. It was extraordinary, sure, but it just looked so malplaced. Like it belonged in the middle of Stonehenge or something. Engraved on its smooth, glasslike surface was a single tribal eye.

"Penny!" Jason suddenly called from the front door. "You found it!"

I smiled and walked over to him. I could see two figures crowding the doorway behind him, and as I approached Jason stepped aside to let them through.

"Penny," Jason said. "Meet my parents. Mom, dad, this is Penny."

I smiled and reached out my hand awkwardly. Mr. Myers grabbed it firmly, and gave it a rigorous shake. He was a tall, rugged, rather handsome man in his mid-fifties.

"Pleased to meet you, Penny," he smiled. "I'm Gerald. Jason's told us all about you."

Mrs. Myers took my other hand and shook it gently. She looked thin and fragile, maybe a little bit older than Mr. Myers. I felt rather trapped standing there with a parent in either hand. At least they seemed welcoming. Too welcoming, one could even say.

"I'm Vivian," she said. "So wonderful to finally meet you."

I thanked them both, and followed them inside. The house was nice, quite spacious, a normal family home by any standards. I tried to spot any abnormalities, like strange religious ornaments or iconography or some such, but everything looked perfectly dull and clean.

"Dinner's almost ready," Mrs. Myers said. "So please just take a seat ."

The dinner table was set up beautifully, with candles and napkins folded like swans and all manner of lovely decorations. Jason pulled out a chair and beckoned for me to sit down in it.

Mr. and Mrs. Myers disappeared into the kitchen, and I took Jason's hand and smiled.

"They don't seem strange at all," I said. "Perfectly normal."

"It's still early," he laughed. "Give it time."

"By the way," I turned my gaze to the window. "What's the deal with the stone?"

Before Jason had the chance to answer, Mr. and Mrs. Myers came back, hazardously balancing a few too many smoking hot pots and pans in their hands.

"Please," I said. "Let me help you."

Mr. Myers chuckled, and gracefully arranged the pots on the table with impressive speed and accuracy.

"I used to work at a restaurant," he said. "30 years. I've got some practise."

Mr. and Mrs. Myers sat down opposite us and

smiled a creepily identical smile.

"So, Penny," Mr. Myers said. "Jason told us you work with computers?"

"Yeah," I smiled. "Software actually."

"One of those eggheads, huh?" he chuckled. "I suppose that's a good occupation."

"Maybe she could take a look at our printer?" Mrs. Myers chimed in. "That darned thing never seems to work."

"Mom," Jason said. "She's not here for work. Leave her alone."

"Oh, I'm sorry," she said. "You're quite right of course. My apologies, Penny."

"It's alright," I said. "I could maybe take a look at it later if you want me to."

They both just kept smiling, silently staring at Jason and me, and at some point it became rather unnerving. Suddenly Mr. Myers got up from his seat and walked over to a cabinet at the far end of the room. He opened a drawer and took something from it, before returning to his seat.

"We have to pray for the meal," Mr. Myers said. "But first, we need you to do something."

I stared at him quizzically as he handed me an adhesive eye patch. My sister used to wear one as a kid to correct her lazy eye, but I just couldn't fathom why he wanted me to wear one now.

"I know it might seem strange," Mr. Myers said. "But please humour us. Wear it over your left eye, and I will explain everything as we go along."

Jason squeezed my hand gently and smiled, and I realised we were getting into the weird religion part of the evening. I shrugged slightly, and took off the wrapper, carefully placing the eye patch over my left eye as instructed.

"Wonderful," Mr. Myers said. "Let us remove the Veil."

I gasped in horror as they all, Jason included, grabbed their left eye in between thumb and index finger, yanked out the eyeball and placed it gently on the table. I knew Jason had an artificial eye, hence the almost in almost normal, but I had no idea the entire family were missing an eye.

"Now," Mr. Myers said. "Let us join hands."

Mr. Myers extended his arm across the table and I nervously did the same. When we were all joined, the three of them lifted their heads and just stared at the ceiling. Anxious and quite weirded out, I resolved to mimicking their behaviour. I don't know how long we held that pose, but I'm guessing roughly five minutes. My hands were shaking, and my neck felt strained, when suddenly Mr. Myers started talking.

I say talking, but that's not really what he did. It was like a deep hoarse croaking sound, like a frog was stuck in his throat and he was desperately trying to cough it up. I could see his neck bulging weirdly as the horrifying noises lowered and rose in pitch in mesmerizing patterns, almost like a shamanistic chant or something. Then, just as sudden as it had started, he stopped, and everyone lowered their heads and let go of each others hands.

"Now," Mr. Myers continued. "Let us feed the Unseeing Eye."

Mr. Myers lifted off the lid on one of the pots, and they each stuck a hand in there. I edged back in my seat uneasily as I realised what was in it. I'm not sure what animal it was from, but I recognize entrails when I see them. They were uncooked and bloody, the slippery squelching repulsive sounds of their hands greedily grabbing them causing my stomach to churn.

What happened next caused me to get up from my seat in horror and disgust.

They were stuffing the bloody dripping entrails into their empty eye sockets, really pushing them in there with their fingers, and moaning creepily while doing so. I edged back until I reached the wall, unable to take my eyes off the vile, ungodly ritual. They kept doing this until the pot was empty, before Mr. Myers put the lid back on, and smiled in my direction.

"Final part, Penny," he said. "Don't worry, I know this all might seem very strange to you."

They all grabbed their eyes from the table, and plopped them back in. I could still hear the horrible squelching sound of the entrails slithering around in there. If I didn't know better, I'd say it sounded exactly like someone...chewing.

"I-I'm sorry," I stuttered. "I ju-just remembered I have an appointment."

I slowly edged from the wall towards the door, never once averting my gaze. I felt sick, repulsed, and utterly horrified, and I just wanted to get the hell out of there.

Mr. Myers smiled. "I understand," he said. "We understand completely."

He got up and walked to the cabinet again, opening another drawer, lifting from it a small cardboard box.

"Take this," he said. "A parting gift. We are so glad you could join us, Penny. You are everything Jason said you'd be."

I'd edged my way to the front door when he approached me, offering me the cardboard box ceremoniously. I grabbed the thing quickly, and gave a fake smile in return.

"So sorry," I said. "I just forgot what day it was."

Mr. Myers chuckled. "No need to apologize. We'll see you again soon, no?""Y-Yes," I said, hurrying out the front door. I walked briskly to my car, ripped off the eye patch, and reversed out of the driveway like a lunatic. I threw one last glance at the house. The three of them were standing in the doorway smiling, waving energetically in my direction.

It's been five hours since I got home. The first thing I did was sit down with a bottle of wine, just staring at the box. It took me two hours and two more bottles to muster up the courage to open it. It contained only one thing. One single item. But it immediately sent shivers down my spine.

An artificial eye.

The thing is, it looks exactly like my eyes. Same

color and everything.

And I don't know what's going on with my left eye. It's been itching something terrible, and it feels swollen and sore. And sometimes, I swear...

I swear I can feel something moving behind it.

THE CURIOUS CASE OF BABY JEANIE

Jeanie was born on a wednesday. I remember this perfectly because her mother died the same day, and her name was Wednesday (named after the day, not the daughter from the Addams Family, nor the nursery rhyme), and I found that to be quite poetic, if not somewhat absurdly ironic. She cried non-stop for hours (Jeanie, not Wednesday; Wednesday died without so much as a whisper) and I couldn't quite figure out how to make that infernal ruckus stop. The nurses were no help at all; too busy mopping up the now bloodied floor, and taking care of my soon-to-be dead wife.

Baby Jeanie didn't have eyes then. By that I mean, they weren't open yet. It's a strange thing to behold when a newborn opens their eyes for the first time; it's like a window to a completely unknown universe, and Jeanie's universe in particular seemed governed by laws that slightly favored multifarious conundrums.

After that initial shock of our first encounter, we soon found our way, baby Jeanie and I. The infernal ruckus gradually faded to a discordant high-pitched screech, invariably causing my ears to bleed, but what can you do? As a parent you must face these challenges with an unflinching smile, bleeding orifices or not; it shall remain our perpetual responsibility to provide our offspring with the best possible chance for survival.

It didn't take long for me to realise that baby Jeanie was special. Her terrifying blue eyes would burrow into my mind, requesting the oddest of favors from inside my head. Even as a tiny, mostly stationary baby all she had to do was shoot me a glance, and I'd come running to do her bidding. Before her intellect developed it'd be the silliest of demands of course. A rattle, a change of nappies, some formula, fresh blood from the cat. All things I could hastily present to her without too much of a fuss.

We never really settled on a name for her, so for the first few months I just called her baby Wednesday (after her mother, not the day). My wife suffered a cruel affliction of both body and mind for the majority of the incubation period, and as such our main concern throughout would remain her failing health. I adored the name though. Baby Wednesday. It felt like a lovely homage to my deceased wife. Baby Jeanie, however, did not agree.

One particular night, I believe a monday, I awoke in the pitch-blackness staring into those dreadful sapphire peepers; Jeanie, barely two months old, had crawled out of her crib, up to my king size bed, onto my chest, now gripping my mustache at either side with unparalleled strength. I swallowed deeply and remained motionless.

"Father dearest," Jeanie spoke. "I wish to inform you that my name henceforth shall be Jeanie. I will no longer answer to the name Wednesday, baby Wednesday, or any combination thereof."

Then she crawled back into her crib again, and I could sleep peacefully knowing she'd found her name, which in turn meant that I didn't have to. That was the first time Jeanie spoke, and curiously enough it wouldn't happen again for several years (or months, depending on how you see it). I suppose she really didn't have to verbally announce her wishes after that. If she wanted anything, she'd just slither into my mind and leave enough breadcrumbs for me to understand.

After the aforementioned night Jeanie grew up fast. And I mean that quite literally; in a couple of months she had matured into the brain and body of a seven year old. You might raise an eyebrow or two at this statement, and rightfully so, but rest assured: there remains a simple explanation for this seemingly preternatural blossoming. It's just not the answer you'd expect.

I came to see in my little girl something sinister. Now I was no parenting expert by any means; but even I had to conclude that something wasn't quite right about her. She was four months old by my count (and about seven or so biologically) when she bit off a limb. Her jaw stretched unnaturally as she chomped down on the babysitters toes, and after the incident we came to the mutual agreement that perhaps a babysitter wasn't such a good idea; it'd be best if I just quit my job and became her servant full time.

School wasn't easy for her, of course. Too many distractions. Too many limbs. And she was the youngest in her class too, having barely turned six months (or twenty-six weeks, which strangely enough seems to be a socially acceptable way of recounting your child's age). She never got into any trouble per se, but I could tell she was exhausted by the end of school days. Too many minds to wreak havoc on I suspected. Poor little thing. I'd feed her whatever limb I didn't need at the time; a tip of my finger, sometimes half a toe, and she'd drift off suckling on the open wound, bathed in the soothing warmth of our fireplace. Those were good times. Innocent times.

She wouldn't allow me to be alone in my head for too long during these trying times. And why complain? Feeling the soft, creeping tendrils of your firstborn squirming around in your brain can be quite comforting, and even when the unimaginable pain forced my body into violent seizures, I could always count on sweet Jeanie to keep me company until the inevitable darkness of unconsciousness swallowed me.

But every once in a while I'd resurface from the abyss with an unconstrained mind. It wouldn't last long, maybe five minutes, but in that time I experienced how life would look without the unending love of my daughter. And it was dreadful. Filled with autonomy and decisions, the world suddenly appeared chaotic and disordered. I'd do strange things in these fleeting moments. Things I'd soon come to regret. Like the time I called nurse O'Sullivan.

It was a Tuesday afternoon. Jeanie would have been about five months, or twenty-one weeks. She was still sleeping when I emerged from my slumber; I could always tell by the look in her eyes when she was in the other place. Those aquamarine globs would appear quite dull and lifeless, and she'd stop breathing. For some inexplicable reason I grabbed the phone, and dialled a seemingly random sequence of numbers.

"Hello?" Siobhan O'Sullivan said. "To whom am I speaking?"

"Evening madam," I whispered. "I must be brief. Do you remember my wife, Wednesday?"

Nurse Siobhan O'Sullivan was one of three nurses present when Jeanie and Wednesday traded places. She even attended the funeral, and seemed overly concerned with my well-being throughout the somber affair. I kept reminding her I was a single father now, and that I would not leave the memory of Wednesday tainted.

"The day?" Siobhan asked.

"A patient, my wife," I said. "Surely you remember Wednesday."

"I do apologize, sir," she seemed rather reluctant to indulge me. "What was her surname?"

"Friday," I said. "Wednesday Friday."

Her father's name was Friday (named after the

day, not the fictional character from Robinson Crusoe), and honoring certain traditions we decided to assume the name as our own upon our marriage. It seemed only fitting.

"Ah, why of course," Siobhan chirped. "Wednesday Friday, how could I ever forget."

"Quite," I said.

"It's been so very long, mr. Friday," she said. "But I remember."

"Whatever do you mean?" I asked. "It's been but five months?"

She fell silent then. I could hear her breathing, like a chill wintery breeze, pausing every once in a while, assumedly to regain her composure.

"Grisly affair that," she said eventually. "One that stays with you."

"I'm sure," I said. "What do you recall of her affliction?"

"The tumor?" she asked. "It caught us by surprise. Never seen anything like it."

"Come again?"

"It ate her up," her voice trembled. "Nothing left in her but rot and decay."

Before my thoughts could form into something comprehensible, I was abruptly cut short by Jeanies violent gaze. She required my assistance forthwith, and I felt it necessary to end the conversation with Siobhan O'Sullivan post-haste.

"Mr. Friday," Siobhan said with utmost affection and care, "It's been more than five months. It's been ten ye-"

"That's quite enough, father dearest," Jeanie interrupted. "I demand from you undivided attention at once."

A child's needs must come first. That's a parents only decree. I threw the phone into the fireplace, and we sat back and listened to the erratic crackling of plastic and glass melting. It was in those moments of warmth and affection that I would remember how much of a miracle Jeanie truly was.

Wednesday (my late wife, not the day) was barren. I was infertile. We weren't meant to create life. But life somehow found us. Who knows where it all started? Perhaps it was always fated. Perhaps it was Wednesday's mental affliction that brought Jeanie to us. My wife used to journey the universe in her dreams. Cover vast distances in her mind, visit places unknown to God and mankind alike. Meet strange unliving things. Sometimes she'd talk to them in her sleep. Whisper strange names and sing their praise. She had a wonderful voice, Wednesday. Harmonious like a forgotten cemetery, cheery as a void sun, vibrant like the end of all things.

She'd forget things as a result of her travels, and soon after the memory loss started she'd slip into her affliction and surface no more. Lost in the endless expanse of the forever. I always imagined her joyfully traversing eternity, even after her death. Almost like Jeanie set her free.

"Do you love me, father dearest," Jeanie echoed

in my mind.

"Unquestionably," I said.

"You know now how this will end?" she asked.

"Yes."

"Be not afraid, father dearest," her tendrils caressed my amygdala. "You have served me longer than any other. You shall soon know rest."

I just nodded. There is no pain or regret in passing when you leave behind an eternal legacy. Jeanie will embrace life without me, of this I am certain. She will embrace it, and snuff it out of existence, as is her way.

If you see Jeanie, please take care of her. That's all I ask of you. Take her in. Hold her tight. Let the glory of those azure orbs creep into your mind and you shall know hardship no more. You will become the servitor she deserves. The servitor she needs. And that is our only function as parents; fulfill our child's every need, even if that need is to devour the entirety of creation. Who are we to enforce what path they choose?

Jeanie is ready to move on. My body cannot handle her much longer. It is foul and and rotten and gangrenous. Funny word, gangrenous. Derives from the latin word gangraena, and the greek gangraina. Interestingly enough it has nothing to do with color. Isn't that something? Just means putrefaction of tissues.

And with that said I feel whole again. Hollow in body perhaps, but my spirit runneth over. It is almost time for me to go.

Time at last to explore eternity with my Wednesday.

SIX DEATHS, SIX FUNERALS, SIX LIVES

Death.

You can't escape it.

You know the word intimately. You've known it since you were old enough to think. Old enough to imagine loss.

But the true meaning will elude you until you've witnessed it firsthand.

Until you've known grief so strong it threatens to destroy you. To destroy everyone around you. To dismantle everything you are, leaving you a soulless, hollow husk.

If you've been there, to that place of anguished sorrow, like I have, then you'll know. Know why I did the things I did. Understand the choices I made. You'll come to realize that you would have done them too. Without hesitation. Without regret.

And, if you had to, you would do them all over again.

May 14th 2002 - R.I.P Grandpa Miles

My grandfather, or just grandpa Miles, was the kindest, gentlest man I knew. He taught me how to fish, how to make a fire, how to respect people, not because they demanded it, but because they deserved it. I was seven years old when he fell off the roof, hitting the rocky ground face first. They told me his neck snapped instantly on impact, so at least he wasn't in any pain. But they weren't there. They didn't hear him wheezing, lungs struggling to filter out the excess blood. They didn't see the desperation in his gaze as life slowly slipped away from him.

But I did. I found him. I was there when he died.

December 22nd 2004 - R.I.P Auntie J

Auntie Joanne slipped on the ice. I could have held onto her, but I wasn't strong enough. I remember her beautiful blonde hair disappearing underneath the trailer, and then the unmistakable sound of a body being crushed under unimaginable pressure, followed then by her body sort of bouncing down the street, the trail of blood so vividly contrasted in the sparkling snow.

The crowd gathered so fast. Piercing screams permeating the air. But I couldn't move, her dead eyes staring right at me.

June 3rd 2005 - R.I.P Cousin Johnny

Johnny was auntie Joanne's boy, and my brother and I used to play with him all the time. Really funny guy. Full of life. After auntie died though, he changed. Withdrew into himself. Closed off the world. Couldn't handle the anguish, or the bullying, or the abuse, I suppose. I was right outside his room when I heard the shotgun blast. I didn't know it actually did that, you know. Blow a hole right through the head? Figured it was a myth.

It isn't.

November 10th 2008 - R.I.P Lawrence

Lawrence was my best buddy growing up. We'd do everything together, and I owe so many of my best childhood memories to him. I didn't know, though. I should have. All those bruises and broken bones. Signals, red flags. When he didn't show up for school one day I went to look for him. I guess I missed him by mere minutes. It was so bloated, you know, his face. Like a big, blue, bulbous, amorphous shape. They later said it was internal bleeding. He always bled on the inside, my friend Lawrence.

I heard his father killed himself in jail. His mom drank herself to death. So much grief. Dark and ugly.

No real escape.

February 30th 2010 - R.I.P Dad

I was sat in the backseat when my dad lost control of the car. It was entirely avoidable, you know. He was going too fast. In a hurry to get to my brother in the hospital. I remember the exact moment I realised he was dead. The car was upside-down, I was upside-down, and I glanced at my dad, hanging limply from the seatbelts. A jagged piece of metal was sticking out of his throat, and there was this steady, hypnotizing stream of blood dripping from the wound. His mouth was moving, like he was trying to speak, but there was no sound. I've since tried to decipher the movement, transcribing his last, inaudible words.

Help me.

August 10th 2013 - R.I.P Eric

My brother always felt responsible for dad's death. I guess I blamed him too. We all did. We never told him that, of course, but he could tell. He knew. His drug habit had only gotten worse since dad passed. You know, heavier stuff. Addictive stuff. Life-crippling stuff. His girlfriend called me that night. She was out of her mind, hysterical, didn't make any sense. Kept yelling incoherently, crying, sobbing. He was ice-cold when I found him, needle sticking out of his arm, discolored foam at his mouth. His dead eyes filled with sadness and regret.

You can't get away.
Death.
It's always there.
The funeral was heavy shit. Coming from me that's saying something, because I've attended quite a few. My mom broke down crying repeatedly, my little sister looked deathly pale and way too skinny, and I kept fearing she'd collapse and never wake up again. At one point Tracy, my brother's girlfriend - she's the one that called me that night - drunkenly tumbled to the floor, and the priest had to help her up. It was horrible. Bleak, depressing, utterly devastating shit. I couldn't wait for it to be over.

But still I stayed behind.

Long after they'd lowered the coffin, I stood there with Tracy. We didn't say anything. There was nothing to be said. No words that could fill the hollow gap between us. No words that could bring him back, to make everything alright, to justify his death. She sat down in the grass, staring down into the gaping hole in the ground. It's quite poetic you know. Opening a wound in the earth to swallow your loved one.

"You must be getting pretty fed up with these, huh?" a cheery voice called from behind me.

I turned to face the owner of the voice, taken aback by the perceived rudeness of the statement, but had to swallow my disdain once I locked eyes with the stranger. He was tall and tan, long blonde hair, sparkling emerald eyes, clad in a white hoodie and basic jeans. He grinned widely, a slight nod when our eyes met.

"I'm sorry, do I know you?" I asked.

He chuckled heartily. "You sure do," he said. "I'm always around, Logan. Just gotta know how to find me."

"You knew Eric too?" I turned my gaze to the chasm in the earth. Maybe it was one of his scumbag dealers or something, coming to claim old debts from Tracy.

"We met once or twice," the man said. "Always in passing though, never one for idle conversation, your brother."

I nodded weakly. I'd spent years trying to get through to Eric, but nothing ever seemed to help. He was lost to me, lost to the world, and I just wished I could change it somehow.

"You can, you know," the man said cheerily. "Change it. Doesn't have to be this way. Doesn't have to be an endless array of dead loved ones. I mean, it's such a bitch, you know? Can never truly retire that gloomy funeral suit, can you? Always a new one around the corner."

I felt a sudden urge to punch him in the face, but I quickly reconsidered. I don't know why, I guess something told me it would be a really bad idea.

"What do you want?" I spat aggressively. "My brother just died, and I just want to be left alone."

I had to take a step back when he suddenly started laughing. It's like your subconscious can't handle it, you know. When people don't behave the way they should. The way you're taught they should. Some sort of reptile brain defense mechanism I suppose.

"I don't want anything, Logan," he said coldly. "I'm here to give you what you want."

"And what is that?" I asked, edging away from him slowly. Tracy was still on her knees by the grave, and she didn't even seem to register our conversation.

"To save your loved ones, of course," he grinned. "Surely you must be getting sick and tired of churches, headstones, and grief-ridden speeches by now. I can take those away. Well, in a sense anyway."

"What do you mean? How?" I turned to face him again, my mind struggling to make sense of the absurdity of his words.

"Death is purely coincidental most of the time, Logan," he pointed to Eric's grave. "The Butterfly Effect and all that jazz. Flip of a coin, heads or tails. Unseen odds and probabilities. It only takes a nudge to change fates, and I'm a really experienced nudger."

"What the hell are you talking about?" I yelled, momentarily forgetting where I was. "Who the fuck are you?"

He smiled eerily as he placed a hand on my shoulder, his piercing gaze unflinching. "Hey, I get where you're coming from. It's hard to believe. But I can show you, Logan. Do you want me to show you?"

I guess I nodded? I mean, it was involuntary, I'm sure. Just an instinctive reaction to a question I didn't quite understand. But the man obviously saw it as an invitation, because moments later he violently jabbed both his thumbs into my eyes. And I mean into. I could feel them turning to mushy, gooey liquid, the pain so intense that my brain registered it throughout the entirety of my body. I'm certain I screamed. A tormented wail. But I couldn't hear anything. Couldn't feel anything.

But I could see.

"Pay close attention, Logan," the man whispered. "I'm only going to show you this once."

In my mind, or in his mind, or in some fucked up version of someone's mind, I was shown every death I'd witnessed in my rather short life. Except no one died. No one I loved anyway. Just a nudge. That's all it takes. Someone else slipping on the ice instead of my aunt. My brother refusing that first needle that sent him to the hospital. My grandpa watching in horror as the neighbor tumbles off the roof. The same events, just slightly different. Changing fates.

When I came back from the fucked up vision I was on the ground, eyes all fine and solid, no wounds, gooey liquids, or blood, or anything. The man was still there, harrowing over me imposingly, looking down at me with those unflinching green eyes, a perfect smile resting on his lips.

"What do you say, Logan?" he reached out an arm. "Do we have an understanding?"

I stared at it hesitantly. "What exactly are you offering me?" I asked, voice all cracked and shivering.

"Oh, it's quite simple, but I'd love to break it down for you," he said darkly. "Tracy! Tracy dear, come over here."

He beckoned for Tracy to come over, and without saying a word she sauntered closer, eyes locked to the ground, movement all slow and jerky. If I didn't know any better I'd say she wasn't even breathing. That she was a cold, broken, rotting corpse, just like her boyfriend. Just like my brother.

"Six deaths, six funerals," the man said, placing a hand on Tracy's shoulder. "Let's say I give you six lives. Six-six-six. Has a certain ring to it, wouldn't you say?"

"I don't understand…" I murmured quietly.

"Let's put it this way, whenever someone you love is at odds of dying, I'll nudge them the other way. I'll let your true feelings decide who has to go instead. Six times. That's the deal. That's more than anyone gets in a lifetime."

"But how will I know?" I looked up at him, tears streaming from my eyes. "This makes no sense."

"Glad you asked!" he laughed, gaze shifting over to Tracy. "Tracy here will show us. Six deaths that are destined to happen. Six deaths I'll steer away from the one you love most."

He snapped his fingers theatrically, and sat down in the grass next to me. "You gotta tune in to this, man. It's really something."

I still can't revisit that memory without feeling nauseous. Without feeling my stomach churning. It all happened in less than a minute. Less than a second maybe. But it felt so much longer. Some days it feels like I'm still there, watching poor Tracy die six times, repeated perpetually.

First her body shook violently, like something hit it. Bones protruding through skin, mouth, ears, and eyes bleeding. Next, a knife sticking out of her abdomen. I could see her guts hanging there limply, the blood flowing from the wound ceaselessly. Then a loud bang, like a gunshot, bullet wound instantly appearing in the middle of her forehead, a fountain of crimson spraying from it. A smell of burnt flesh permeated the air as her skin suddenly melted away, the exposed flesh and muscles sizzling horribly. An audible thump then, as the entire right side of her skull was flattened, bones shattering, fluids exploding everywhere. Finally, her body was elevated, neck stretching, neck snapping, eyes popping.

Then it was over. An eternity reduced to a second.

Tracy fell to the ground, all the wounds, traumas, broken bones, holes, guts, burnt flesh, snapped neck, all the horror, vanished in an instant. She wheezed heavily, slow, guttural breathing, but appeared relatively unharmed given the circumstances.

"So, do we have an understanding?" the man said, grinning widely.

"We do," I said without hesitation.

"Marvellous," he got up to his feet, and sauntered toward my brother's grave. "You're doing the right thing here, Logan. Never doubt that."

"What about her?" I muttered, pointing to Tracy. "Will she be OK?"

"Don't mind her," he said. "She wants to crawl into the casket with your brother. I'm very intrigued to see if she actually goes through with it."

He threw his head back and laughed heartily. "I'll see you around, Logan," he said, and then he jumped into the gaping wound in the soil.

I checked it before I left.

But he wasn't there.

Death.

Can you escape it?

September 2nd 2015 - My Mom Didn't Die

An elderly driver collapsed behind the wheel, swerving onto the pedestrian walkway. An old lady had dropped her purse right before it happened, and my mom stopped to help her gather her belongings. Had my mom continued walking, she'd be the one crushed by the vehicle, instead of the young teenage girl.

Bones protruding from skin, mouth, ears, and eyes bleeding.

January 16th 2016 - My Sister Didn't Die

They never caught the guy that did it, you know. The back alley stabber. My sister's friend died alone in the darkness. No one heard her screaming. No one heard her crying. She was devastated, my sister. It could have been me, she sobbed in my arms. Apparently her friend was running an errand for my sister. It could have been her. It should have been her.

I met Marina, my future wife, randomly on the street after visiting my sister that day. She hit me (accidentally, or so she claimed) with a brick, and accompanied me to the hospital to get the stitches done. We talked, kissed and fell in love all in one wonderful, magical day.

Life was good.

You can escape.

March 30th 2017 - My Mother and Wife Didn't Die

They were out shopping, the three of them. My wife, my sister, and my mom. Wedding dress. They were looking for a wedding dress. I guess the robber was in the wrong place, at the wrong time. Didn't see the cops parked outside. My sister caught a stray bullet from the shootout. Crimson stained wedding dresses all around. It could have been anyone. But I must have loved her the least.

November 21st 2019 - My Wife Didn't Die

She was only staying there over the weekend. I had a thing at work, and since she was seven months pregnant, she didn't want to be alone. My mom said she'd take care of her. That I didn't need to worry. My mom slept on the couch upstairs, while my wife occupied her bed. I guess she didn't hear the smoke detector.

I guess I loved my wife more.

January 20th 2020 - My Wife Didn't Die

She was heavy, you know. Big old tummy. Almost time now, the doctors told us. It was just one of those things. Random accident. Lost her footing going down a flight of stairs. What was she doing down there anyway? Her stomach took a beating. A real brutal beating. It tears me up, you know. But it's the truth. There's no denying it. I loved her more than I loved our unborn child.

That tiny little cranium just wasn't built to take a beating.

Present Day - My Ex-Wife Won't Die

She blamed herself. Punished herself. I watched as she spiralled into that black place. Pit of despair. Ceaseless depression. I knew then what I had to do. How I could save her. How I could stop it all. I'll leave her this note, this last confession, so that she will understand. Understand that it's all my fault. Not hers.

I love you, Marina. This is not on you.

This is where it was going all along, wasn't it? A gentle nudge from a very experienced nudger, all the while guiding me to this very moment.

I can hear you laughing, you know. I know you're here. But even if I knew, knew all along where it was going, I wouldn't change it. Wouldn't change a thing.

Gloomy funeral suit, finely pressed. Check.

Noose at the ready, solid rope. Check.

A long drop, ending in a brutal snap. Check.
Death.

You can't escape it.
But you can embrace it.

LIVING WITH THE DAVID REYES DISORDER

I have this psychological condition, I guess most would call it a mental disorder, but I just find the word disorder to be shrouded in negativity and misinformation, and to be fair it really doesn't bother me that much. A condition on the other hand people seem to treat with respect and understanding, like it isn't my fault, like I was just born with this thing, nothing else to it, you know.

They call it the David Reyes Disorder, or DRD for short. Incidentally, my name is David Reyes, and I'm also the only known person ever diagnosed with the condition. Isn't that strange? I for one always found that very peculiar.

I was diagnosed at age four, after spending weeks and months at a special hospital, then months and years at a very isolated psychiatric facility. My parents would visit, of course, but mostly I spent my days alone with the doctors.

Living with the condition has been a challenge, I'll admit it, but it isn't as bad as people would have you think. In the beginning it was scary and traumatizing because I was too young to understand it, but as I've grown older I've learned to come to terms with it. The human mind is marvellous; there really isn't anything it can't overcome given enough time.

My first episode happened in daycare when I was three. I remember it vaguely as a truly horrible experience, but I can't seem to recollect the exact details anymore. I guess was just too young. I scared the living hell out of everyone, I'll tell you that much, because I was never in daycare again.

The experience I get nowadays is something in between sleep paralysis and extreme psychosis. I can't move, like I'm locked inside my body, and I get these incredibly detailed nightmarish visions, oftentimes accompanied by auditory hallucinations. Usually I will see someone brutally murdered, like ripped to shreds or exploding or gruesomely eviscerated or... well you get the idea. Real gory stuff. Then suddenly it will all be over and the doctors will help me get to sleep and I'll wake up fine and dandy the next morning.

It's the strangest thing though...some days the doctors will visit me real early in the morning, like before the sun comes up, and they'll have this guy with them, some office man dressed in a fine suit and tie. Sometimes I recognize him, sometimes not. Anyway, they sit down and this guy shows me a picture of a person. They'll tell me to focus on the person, like it's someone I should know but I've forgotten about or something. And I will focus as hard as I possibly can, because I want to get better.

But let me tell you...sometimes...

Sometimes I remember the person too well.

And I'll witness their horrible death in my episodes.

And the doctors will smile and tell me how good I've been.

Don't you think that's strange?

ONE-ONE-EIGHT

At dusk I stare into the bleak forest, my eyes transfixed on a specific spot of nothing for hours at a time, never blinking, never thinking. Darkness will eventually devour the tall pine trees, and when the last remnant of colour fades, as will my trance. My eyes will hurt as I slowly regain my senses, and I will remember each moment like a soft vibration in the back of my mind. My arms will be heavy lumbering things, swinging idly by my side. My back hunched and sore, my legs now trembling from exhaustion. I will eventually make my way to bed, and suffer a restless, dreamless sleep. When I wake up, it is like a perpetual mist fading, slowly revealing everything, just a little bit clearer for each passing day.

I've counted fifty-three since it first started. If I recall correctly, there are still sixty-five to go.

My father told me to count. One day, he'd say, I would have to pass on the knowledge, just like he did. He ordered me to watch him as he stood out in the cold, staring into the vast nothing of the forest. And I did. And I counted. I would help him back to bed, his tired eyes now filling with tears, back hunched, legs trembling. I would watch him writhe in silent agony every night, and witness the monumental relief on his face upon waking. This I would do every night, because I knew what would happen if I didn't.

One-one-eight.

Daytime passes like a slowly rising ache, and I will scratch at my forehead anxiously as dusk approaches. Then the ritual will repeat itself, and I will wake with an ever growing sense of clarity.

I never knew my grandfather. He died when my father was young, the circumstances never revealed to me as a boy. But my father would tell me stories from the old country that his father had told him. Dark, disturbing tales of grotesque nature, their ultimate meaning largely lost on me at the time. Tales of profane treachery and ceremonies of depravity. Stories of murder and torture, each one more horrendous than the last. As a boy I never understood how my father could find it in him to torment me with these ghastly anecdotes, but as I grew older I would eventually come to suspect the meaning.

They were cautionary tales.

On day fifty-nine the training began. Every day after I would follow my father as he set off into the forest, not returning until dusk approached once more. We would follow the trail to the lake, and he would explain to me in vivid detail what was to come, and what must be done. Every day, the same trail, the same talk. He would show me where it had to happen, and we would stop there, at that exact spot, and train for hours. There was no room for failure, he'd say, because failure would mean the end of everything.

No. Not just cautionary tales. Legacies.

I am my father now. The legacy, the ritual, the tales. Every night now I must relive the moment. I have to. There is no room for failure. A gentle rustle of a branch. Sombre snowflakes floating slowly towards the frozen soil. A smell of death lingering in the cold air, like a harrowing shadow of what is to come. I find myself closer and closer to the edge of the forest, drawn inexplicably to the spot of nothing. And as my body expulses my mind, I drift back to the past and remember.

One-one-eight.

On the last day we sat silently by the frozen lake, facing each other like living fur-clad statues. The evergreen giants surrounding the clearing waved their branches in unison patterns as the cold wind ravaged through the snowscape. We didn't need to talk. There was nothing left to say. I could hear the sound of drums in the distance. A deep, slow, steady, hypnotizing beat. My father sat in deep concentration, eyes closed, head raised to the sky. A gentle stream of blood running down his forehead and into his open mouth. It was almost time.

My joints are sore and cold, and I often feel my mind slipping through the cracks of reality. It longs for somewhere else. But there are still months ahead, and I am not prepared. There is much yet to do. As dusk approaches, I walk out to the edge of the forest.

Somewhere in the depths of that dark haven yearns my being, and I cannot resist it. I will not. Violently I scratch at my forehead, trying desperately to imagine that ungodly night so long ago.

And then it comes.

Catching my breath, so tired, I quickly glance up at the tall gaunt figure of my father beside me. Clutching erratically at my shoulders, struggling to stay on his feet, he staggers to the side of the trail, a look of pain and desperation in two of his eyes, the third now but a bloody mess. A deep gash in the back of his left thigh, a stark reminder of the true nature of this place, renders him incapable of a steady pace, and we are forced to stop at irregular intervals to rest. The snow falls rapidly around us, the wind now at a strong gale. The trail can no longer be seen, covered now by an ever betraying blanket of white. But we know. We could find our way to the frozen lake blindfolded if need be. And in a sense, we are blind now.

In the distance we hear it.

The forest is awake. No longer moving in unison, each branch now reaching down towards us, like unholy skeletal fingers, grasping violently as we brush past them. The inaudible drip-drip-drip of crimson from my fathers forehead now covering his fur. Behind us we leave an ever increasing trail of blood, sweet, warm and noticeable. We can hear it approaching. The deep, slow, steady, hypnotizing beat of the black heart in pursuit. Darkened tendrils creep up from the snow-covered ground, coiling themselves around the massive trunks of the trees, pulsating in a feverish rhythm as it pumps its lifeforce through them. It has now become the forest.

Then, with the very last of our strength, we push through the grasping claws of the branches, landing face down before the frozen lake. Crystallized snow glimmers eerily upon its surface, an angelic contrast to the utter darkness that surrounds it.

Minutes pass as we lie there, my lungs now practically bursting through my chest. Somehow I am able to get up, legs aching and shaking, hands swinging idly by my side. My father writhing in silent agony from his wounds, still on the ground mere inches from the seeking branches. I stagger towards him, dragging him onto his feet. The beating of the black heart now sounds like deep echoing cracks of thunder. It approaches. Slowly we make our way across the lake, my father, barely able to walk, covering our rear.

We are halfway across when I hear the ice cracking below my feet.

As I turn around, I see my father disappearing beneath the ice, his arms flailing to the side, desperately trying to get a hold of anything. Adrenaline pumps through me again, and I muster enough strength to rush towards the gaping hole in the lake, grabbing hold of his arm just before he is lost to the depths. I am barely able to hold on, let alone get him to safety, and all around me I hear the echoing thunder of the black heart steadily approaching. I remember struggling for what felt like minutes, before my father somehow got both his arms over the ice, now just a dangling torso above the freezing water. He smiles at me then, and a monumental relief seems to wash over him.

This is it, he says. This is what we've been training for.

I nod softly, tears running down my face. The darkness is engulfing us. Well beyond the edge of the forest by now. The black heart but seconds away, it's steady beat now a deafening bang. I hesitate briefly. No amount of training can ever prepare you for this.

It's alright, he says. It is our legacy. We were born for this.

My eyes hurt as I brush away the tears. My thoughts now nothing but chaos, my body a frail lethargic frame, shivering and pathetic. But his smile comforts me, brings me strength, resilience. I nod again, this time firmly, and carefully circle around to his back. The darkness now surrounds us, tendrils slithering along the snow, inching ever closer, the black heart just moments away. I grab my father by the head, hunching down I kiss him gently where the third eye once was. Slowly I unsheath my hunting knife, letting it rest momentarily by his left ear. I stare into the blackness, and within the swirling amorphous mass I can see it. A specific spot of nothing. The black heart of the woods. Through gritted teeth I snarl at it, curse it, hate it, and with a swift move of precision, only made possible through months of tireless training, I slit my fathers throat from ear to ear.

This burden, legacy, I have carried with me all my life. I knew the day would come when the knowledge must be passed on. And so I have spent a lifetime preparing for it.

My family brought the thing with them when they left the old country. A dark stowaway, a halfway forgotten remnant of the ancient ways. It cannot live here, you see. It cannot survive on its own. It will devour everything, unsatisfied, hungry, forever dying, mad and alone. We brought it here, and so we must be the keepers. Whenever it awakes, we must call for it, lure it back to its makeshift prison, before it ascends to its old godlike self. On the eve of its return we must sacrifice onto it one of our own, and watch them both sink to the bottom of the lake.

A son must murder the father. These are the rules of old.

I stagger weakly back from the edge of the forest, heading towards the porch, my son by my side, supporting me as best he can. We have been here for the better part of a year now, ever since I took him from his mother. She can never know why. My son, now twelve, understands this. It took a few months, but I shared with him the tales of the old country, and slowly he began to accept. But I have yet to tell him everything. In a few days we will walk the trail to the frozen lake.

And we will begin the training.

And I will tell him at last.

One-one-eight days from the first dusk you must be ready.

Ready to cut my throat.

MONSTERS DON'T ALWAYS HIDE UNDER YOUR BED

At one point we all knew there lived a monster under our bed. Or in our closet. This wasn't something you believed. It was the cold, hard truth. You never ran to your parents hysterically yelling "I think there's a monster under my bed", nor did you unaffectedly state "I believe there to be a monster in my closet." There is. There is a monster under my bed. There is a monster in my closet.

I, for one, never had any doubt. Wherever I went, wherever I slept, a monster came with me. It just had this annoying habit of never staying in one place.

I guess I was a nervous child. Everything seemed to scare me, especially when it was dark. I hated the dark. You can never really know what hides there, just outside the limits of your own eyes. It can be anything. It can be nothing. Sometimes the nothing is worse, because it means you're all alone. That no one really cares.

We lived alone, my father and I. On the very last house on Far Fletcher St., right on the edge of the vast forest. My mom died or left us, my father was never really clear on that, and he was forced to raise me alone. We don't need anyone else, he'd say. They'll just try to fix what ain't broken.

I was six and a half, almost to the day, when my monster became real. I mean, to me it was real all along, but to the world it had remained hidden. I was counting the days to my birthday. I'd always do this. 365 days, 366 on a leap year, all on catalogue in my head. It was the only day I felt free, the only day I'd get to see other kids. My father would take me to town, and we'd celebrate by eating a burger or pizza, and I'd play in the ball pit, and feel the smiles and joy and warmth of the other children. Heaven.

"We ain't like them," my father would say when I asked why I he wouldn't let me have friends, why he wouldn't let me see other people. "They don't understand us."

It was late fall when it happened; the few decaying leaves left hugging the branches doing so by pure willpower, and the night was freezing cold. I'd tucked myself in real good, my night light switched off because my father didn't like it on, and I was desperately trying to fall asleep before the darkness swallowed me and the monster came. It would always come. My body was hurting. It was always hurting, which only made it that much harder to drift off.

But I guess I must have succeeded, because I can't really remember much until the noises woke me up. I didn't like noises at night, not even the ones I could easily identify, so I quickly hid under my covers, whimpering and crying.

There were voices. Screams. Like someone was trying to break down the front door. Glass shattering. Wood cracking. I covered my ears and started humming to myself. Calming tunes. Melodies I'd heard on the radio. I guess I was trying to drown the nightmare. Swallow the pain of not knowing. In many ways that was always my worst fear; that feeling of dread you'd get from being left in the dark, of having no control.

I can't tell exactly how long I stayed under my covers, desperately trying to ignore whatever was going on. Minutes? Hours? I'm guessing at least half an hour. All I know is that at some point the noises stopped, and I carefully stuck my head out, the place suddenly haunted by dead, horrifying silence. I didn't want to move. Didn't want to breathe.

Didn't want to know what had happened.

Then I heard the footsteps. Slow, steady, heavy. The unmistakable creaking of the old wooden stairs followed, and within seconds I could hear them down the hall just outside my bedroom.

"Are you awake, sweetie," my father whispered hoarsely from the doorway.

I don't know how I felt at that point. My mind was racing, and my heart felt like it was beating outside of my chest. Seeing that harrowing shadow in my door, regardless of who it was, sent shivers down my spine. Memories flooding back.

"Ye-yes," I muttered weakly.

The door opened wide, and he stepped into the room. He looked different, but I couldn't really see him clearly in the vague light of the hall. He took a few heavy steps closer, and sat down at the edge of my bed.

"The noises scared you, huh?" he whispered, "Don't worry. It was just the wind."

He was sweating profusely. Large drops falling like rain onto the hardwood floor. Thump. Thump. Thump. He had this strange expression on his face. Like he was scared, horrified. I pulled the covers up to my nose the moment I noticed it.

"I'm fine," he said, "Don't be scared. You don't have to be scared anymore."

The light hit his eyes as he turned to me, and I could somehow read in them that he was telling the truth. They didn't match his horrible expression at all; radiating warmth and care, a soft, almost sad, gaze.

"You shouldn't be afraid of monsters," he tried to smile, "They can be beaten. Destroyed. Punished. It isn't like the books or the movies. Monsters will always lose."

I nodded confusedly, not quite knowing how to react. He seemed so different to me, but I couldn't really put a finger on why. I was just a kid, you know; a child. Six years is nothing. It's like you've hardly even existed. And for me it was even worse; I'd only ever really existed in a vacuum, sheltered from anything but that house and my father.

"Well, I'll let you get back to sleep," he stood up, "I have a feeling tomorrow's gonna be a good day."

With slow, steady steps he walked back to the door. Just as he was about to cross the threshold, he dropped something. Something wet. It landed on the floor with a disgusting squelch.

"Whoopsie," he whispered, "Oh well, you can keep that. Let it be a reminder. A trophy."

He gently stepped over whatever he dropped, and I listened intently as the footsteps faded, until finally there was nothing but dead silence and darkness again. But for some inexplicable reason I wasn't afraid anymore. It was like a veil had been lifted, and for the very first time I realised I could be in control. That I could master the nightmares.

I drifted off the moment I closed my eyes. I've never slept better. Not before, not since. A perfect, calm, dreamless, all-encompassing sleep.

And I woke up to a good day, just like he said.

I stepped over the pond of blood on the hardwood floor at the edge of my bed, and tippy-toed to the doorway, bending down to carefully inspect the thing he'd dropped the night before.

I guess I must have known. Deep down, I mean. Not just a thought or a fleeting feeling, but really known. That it wasn't really him. That's the only reason I can think of. Because there was no fear, no emotions but relief and calmness, as I gently lifted the bloody, lumpy, sticky remains of my father's face and held it out before me. A hideous, crudely carven mask.

A reminder.

A trophy.

And now they'd know. What I'd known all these years. Know what he really was.

A monster hiding in plain sight.

THE PAVLOVIAN PIGGY

I don't dine out anymore. It's expensive. There's people there. You have to use cutlery. The food has weird, foreign names. Pommes? What the hell is a Pommes? You can't go in your jammies. All excellent reasons for staying home with your microwave dinner. I usually buy the ones labelled gourmet. That's french for tasty.

But I wasn't always like this. Back in the day I frequented the fine dining scene weekly. Don't get me wrong, I was never a feinschmecker about it. That's german for being a snob. No, I just sometimes preferred the cuisine (french for food) of the local restaurants over my own rather disastrous attempts at cooking.

That, and I really enjoyed showing off.

Especially when I was with Jennifer. Jennifer had this particular je nes sais quoi (french for I don't fucking know) quality that made me question myself and my abilities daily. She was a eclectic, electric, eccentric, eloquent, exotic, and (I was hoping) erotic, and I found myself struggling to meet her ever-evolving standards. She despised banalities, not once realising the irony of what she was; the poster-girl for hipster clichés.

I didn't care of course. I thought she was the coolest thing since the Beastie Boys, and the indeterminate nuances of her hair color, mixed with the haphazard placement of her body piercings, had me head over heels for her. She was obnoxious. Edgy. Self-absorbed. Pseudo-intellectual. Pretentious. All excellent qualities to look for in a potential partner.

So when a buddy of mine at work, Vic, God Bless His Soul (he's not dead, he's just still stuck working the same shitty dead-end job), mentioned something called a pop-up restaurant, and how fresh and hip and trendy it was, I immediately knew I simply had to bring Jennifer there for a date. I couldn't call it a date, of course. That would be too mundane. Too label-ly. Maybe a food courting? Or a cuisine carnage? Brunch with Benefits? I'd figure something out.

"So, where's this place?" I asked Vic, "What's it called?"

"You don't get it," he said, "It's a pop-up restaurant. No one knows where it's gonna be, until, you know, it's there."

It was such a weird concept to me, but I guess that's why the hipsters were all over it. It was different. Exciting. Utterly inconvenient and ridiculously overpriced. According to Vic, this place would pop up every week or so, usually in or around abandoned, condemned buildings. They had no web page, no social media presence, no advertising beforehand whatsoever. The word would spread once someone found it, and they would serve customers for six-hundred and sixty-six minutes (yeah, I know) before closing.

The Pavlovian Piggy.

"That's a weird fucking name, isn't it?" I eyed Vic suspiciously, "You sure you're not just fucking with me?"

"Look, places like that, I mean, high-end, or off-the-grid stuff," he said, "always have weird-ass names like that. The Illicit Inuit. The Dalek Llama. The Peruvian Pervert. The Pavlovian Piggy."

I mean, he wasn't wrong. If there's one thing rich people and hipsters can agree on, it's the notion that if it isn't absurdly unique in every way, it's not worth your time. I asked him to put his ear to the ground, and let me know as soon as the place popped up. In the meantime I had to convince Jennifer that I was a person she'd want to spend more than a few minutes alone with.

Now, I'm not a strong believer in luck or fate or destiny as anything but statistical anomalies, but this next part had me questioning how the universe really works for quite a few months. I was walking home after working the late shift with Vic, just a few blocks, and decided to take a shortcut through an alley I'd normally never set foot in at night. Why? I have no idea. I guess I was preoccupied, rigorously fashioning my would-be conversation with Jennifer in my head. As I passed a particularly heinous dumpster, a glowing neon-light suddenly bathed me in a horridly garish pink. Dazed and confused I stood there blinking, reading the erratically pulsating sign over and over again.

The Pavlovian Piggy.

"This can't be fucking real," I muttered incoherently.

But it was. A neon sign depicting a pig being stabbed repeatedly with a two-pronged fork. I wouldn't call it tasteful per se (that's latin for as such), but it definitely captured the essence of a pig getting stabbed, I'll give it that, and I found the blood squirting from the pig's back a particularly nice touch. I kinda just slouched around for a few minutes, nervously peeping into the darkened entrance every once in a while. I'm not sure what I was expecting. But it certainly wasn't what happened.

"Steve," a weirdly high-pitched male voice suddenly called, "Come on in. We've been expecting you."

I don't know if it was the shock of hearing my name, or the sight of that stubby little bald man lurking in the doorway, but I let out a rather effeminate shriek and stumbled back clumsily.

"Ho-How do you know my name?" was all I could muster given the circumstances.

"It says so right there," he pointed to my name tag, "Hi, I'm Steve."

I let out a sigh of relief, moments later realising that wasn't all he had said. "Wait, you are expecting me?" I eyed the vague silhouette suspiciously.

"Yes," he chuckled, "We're always expecting someone. Please, Steve, do come in. You're our first guest this fine evening, thus you are rewarded with the Grand Tour."

He beckoned for me to follow him, and after a few moments of hesitation, I bit my lip, swallowed deeply, and carefully edged my way past the cramped doorway.

"I am Armand," he smiled creepily, "Head Chef, and sole proprietor of this fine establishment. Please, let me show you around."

I didn't know what to say, so I didn't say anything; just dutifully sauntered behind the strange man down a poorly-lit flight of stairs. When he stopped before a really shady-looking steel door, I was really starting to question his motives.

"Hey, man, you know, I'm kind of in a hurry," I mumbled, "So maybe, you know, another time?"

"Steve, Steve, Steve," he turned to look at me, "It's quite alright. I know this is, how do you say it, different, but I assure you, there's nothing but wonder and amazement behind this door."

He grabbed the handle, and with an unbelievably loud screeching sound the door pulled open. I squinted like crazy into the darkness of the room beyond, but couldn't see anything but indistinct, amorphous shapes.

"Do you wish to invite someone to join you?" Armand asked, "Word travels fast, so you better do it now."

"Yes," I said, the thought of Jennifer warming all

the right parts of my body, "Can I text them now?"

"Here," he said, "Let me. There's a rather complex password, and I wouldn't want you to misspell it."

I handed him the phone, and he started typing away in a frenzy. I turned my attention to the room. What on earth was hidden in there? Tables? Chairs? A kitchen? Waldo? Without really noticing, I had moved closer, my head now slowly reaching inside.

"Go on, take a peek," Armand said, "This place is for you, and you alone."

"What the fuck is that supposed to me-"

Before I could finish the sentence I was pushed into the pitch-black room forcefully, barely able to recover before plummeting head-first into the solid concrete floor. I rolled around for a good ten seconds before I heard the sinister screeching of the door, followed by a deafening sound as it slammed shut.

"Hey!" I yelled hysterically. "Let me out! I can't see shit in here!"

I'm not sure if you've ever been locked in a previously unknown location, engulfed by pitch-darkness, but here's what usually follows; blindly running about, flailing of arms, desperate screams, lots of pain as you bump into unseen objects, then, after a while, defeated capitulation, tears, rolling yourself into a sobbing, inconsolable ball in a randomly chosen corner.

"Steve," a crackling voice beckoned from somewhere in the darkness, "The Show is about to start. Please turn your attention to the Scene."

I failed to locate the source of the voice, partly because it remained obscure, but mostly because of the light suddenly beaming through a window at the far side of the room. It was large, maybe 6x6 feet, and it looked completely out of place. I edged closer, sweat now dripping down my forehead into my eyes.

It is hard to explain exactly why I was so taken aback by what I saw in the room beyond the window. It could have been Armand, the stubby little bald fucker standing by a stove at the far end, waving at me theatrically. Or it could have been the naked man sitting on what appeared to be a makeshift kitchen counter in the middle of the room.

"Welcome," the crackling voice boomed, "To the Pavlovian Piggy."

Armands lips moved moments before I could hear the voice, and I quickly realised he was speaking into a microphone, addressing me directly from the other room. I peered around frantically, looking for the hidden speaker, but my surroundings were still mostly veiled by the dark.

"You see," Armand said, "Our Experience isn't only about the food. It's about the Journey, the Preparation, the Art. Life is nothing without the Art of Things."

"You sick little fuck!" I yelled, slamming my fists into the window, "LET ME OUT!"

I noticed an indistinct shadow moving in the room, and Armand briefly turned his attention towards it. He nodded vaguely, and a broad, wicked smile manifested on his lips.

"Ah," Armand said, his gaze now locked on me, "It seems we have our first order of the evening. Marvellous!"

He picked up a tiny object from the counter and raised it above his head. It wasn't until I heard the vague tinkling sound that I realised what it was. A small bell.

"And thus," Armand exclaimed, "begins the Pavlovian Experience."

For a moment nothing happened. My gaze darted all around the room, desperately trying to find a source of distress. There were plenty. Armand, knives, axes, saws, a naked, apathetic man.

"Nononono," I murmured, realising suddenly what was going on, "Nononono, STOP! STOP IT!"

I slammed my fists into the window, tried to kick it, throw my body into it; but it wouldn't budge. Armand just laughed; weird, high-pitched snorts crackling forth from the hidden speaker.

"Just watch him," he said, "It is art. Pure, raw, unfiltered art."

The naked man was wielding a large butcher's knife in his right hand, and with slow, methodical movement he was slicing into his own thigh. Blood ran from the wound in streams, dripping down into metal trays below. He remained completely calm, unfazed by the horror of it, and his face never once changed from that blank, indifferent expression. This continued for minutes, until finally he ripped from his thigh a large chunk of meat, of which he gently handed to Armand.

"And now for the cooking," Armand smiled at me, "That's the boring part."

I slumped down on the cold concrete floor, body drained of energy, mind empty, soul tainted. I couldn't cry. There were no more tears. I'd vomited all over the room, the place now a horrible stinking cesspool of despair. I could hear the sizzling sound of the frying pan, Armand whistling a merry tune, my own heart beating in uneven, frantic intervals.

"Next order," Armand sang, "We need something different."

I heard the bell tinkling again, soon followed by the indescribable, gruesome sound of a knife slowly cutting into human flesh. I couldn't watch. Buried my face in my hands. Another sound; a sharp, violent jerk, indicated without a doubt that a new bloody piece of meat changed hands.

"Steve," Armand said playfully, "You simply must watch. It is a once-in-a-lifetime opportunity!"

I feel sick just thinking about it. My stomach churns as I'm writing this. But I have to be truthful, or else what's the point? There's nothing I would love more than to tell you that I didn't. That I never again let my eyes wander to that room. But I'd be lying.

Every once in a while I'd look up, cued by the detestable tinkle of that bell. There was only stomach acid left to throw up, but I'd retch and convulse on the floor regardless; the sight of the willing, living dish bringing new, unthinkable waves of nausea for every missing pound of flesh. He was covered in blood and bleeding wounds now, more dead than alive; yet still he kept slicing, cutting, ripping, tearing.

Armand would tease me, prod me with his words, knowing full well that I, too, was now a part of his grotesque pavlovian art-piece, woefully unable to ignore the macabre magnum opus transgressing before me. I was forced, by my own twisted, conditioned mind, to watch in disgust and horror and...perverse amazement, as that poor, helpless man cut himself to death, one sinister tinkle after another.

Did it last six-hundred and sixty six minutes? Did it take him that long to die? I honestly don't know. I passed out repeatedly, only to awaken screaming hysterically, terrified by the desperate and bestial nature of my own howls. How many times? Too many to count. The last thing I remember, now etched into my mind forever, was watching the mutilated remains of that man collapsing into the blood-filled trays on the floor, accompanied by Armand's insane high-pitched voice.

"The Pavlovian Piggy is now closed!"

I must have been out for hours. My head was spinning, my body felt like I'd gone twelve rounds against a gorilla, and my eyes were hardly even operational. I squinted around disoriented, before it dawned on me where I was. I stumbled to my feet, walking around in circles, trying to make sense of my surroundings.

I was still in that room, but the door was open. I turned around, staggered towards the window, the ominous light still shining through it, but to my utter disbelief it was...spotless. Clean and empty. No stove. No kitchen counters. No knives or axes. No blood. No mutilated body. No Armand.

"Fucking impossible," I muttered weakly.

And it was. But I was in no shape to question anything, let alone investigate the disappearance of a murder/suicide-kitchen. I just wanted to get the hell out of there, forget it ever happened, never talk about it ever again. Maybe, just maybe, I'd fool myself into believing just that; that it was a dream, a horrible nightmare, a vivid hallucination.

I stumbled through the door, barely able to stand upright, falling to my knees like a sack of shit as I passed the threshold. But there, on the ground, right in front of me; my phone. I grabbed it, desperately scrolling through a bunch of unread messages, all from Jennifer. I felt the sickness returning, my empty stomach convulsing in violent spasms.

J<3: I'll be there asap.

J<3: Where r u? I'm outside.

J<3: Inside now. PW worked.

J<3: Fuck u Steve. Where r u?

J<3: Fuck u for standing me up. Eating without you.

J<3: Mmmm. Fucker.

J<3: Food was delicious. Fucking amazing. U missed out shitbag. Fuck u.

WIGGLE YOUR TOES

"Could you wiggle your toes for me please?"
Wiggle your toes. Such a simple command. Such a basic motoric function. Usually you don't even have to think about it. It just happens instinctively. You hear the word toes, and there they go, all wiggly like.

I...I'm...I'm trying.

Imagine yourself having to work through unimaginable pain, having to focus all your energy on doing something as ridiculously fundamental as wiggling your toes, and still end up failing. It's heartbreaking. Absolutely soul-crushing.

"Try again. Try harder."

I...I can't.

You know there's just more hurt. Physical and mental torture. But you keep pushing, keep trying to wiggle those toes, as if your very life depended on it. In some sense it does. At least it feels like it does. It feels like if you fail this, if you fail again, if those fucking toes don't fucking wiggle, then you might as well give up. Roll over and die.

"Just one more time. Focus, Sasha, give it all

you've got."

I...I'm trying.

Every muscle in your body tenses, contracts, the veins in your forehead pulsating feverishly like bloated worms writhing under your skin; a burning sensation spreading to every fibre of your being as you relentlessly push your will onto every last responding cell, pleading, begging, to just wiggle one fucking toe!

"Ah, wonderful! Great work, Sasha. Really well done."

I...I did it?

You can't imagine the feeling. You really can't. It's like winning the lottery and having sex for the first time on top of the all the money you just won in the lottery. A triumphant, all consuming sensation of accomplishment and joy. But ultimately futile. You know this. I know this. It doesn't change anything. Not really. Just buys you time. How much? A few minutes? Half an hour? More?

"Let's get back to it, shall we?"

N...No...Please...

"Don't worry, Sasha. I just want you to feel it. To tap into every possible pain receptor in your body. It's an integral part of the process, Sasha. I wouldn't need you if you weren't here with me, present, awake, feeling every little poke and prod. That's why they call it art. Art requires sacrifice, dedication, blood, sweat, and tears. Art requires perfection."

I can't lift my head, I can't move my arms or legs, but I can feel everything. The scalpel, the scraping of fingernails against exposed muscles, the pins and needles and cuts into organs and veins. I can see hideous, wrinkly, bloody piles of my own skin. I can see him, gleefully slicing me into thinner and thinner versions of myself.

And I can wiggle them.

I can wiggle my toes.

SWEET DANIEL'S DISTURBING DRAWINGS

I've always been amazed by the seemingly limitless depths of a child's imagination. Their ability to take even the simplest, most rudimentary concept and turn it into something magical and dreamlike has been a fascination of mine for decades. And, in many ways, I believe I owe this obsession to my little brother Daniel and his vividly disturbing drawings.

Daniel was a sweet boy. The sweetest, I dare even say. With his curly golden hair, striking blue eyes, and soft gentle mannerisms, he was every bit as angelic as you'd imagine. He got on well with the other kids, too. Everyone seemed to adore him. A truly blessed child.

So why did the darkness emerge? And from where?

I guess it's hard to say for certain. There were many possibilities. Too many to count. I just know that one day he started drawing. Vague, undefined silhouettes at first, indistinguishable shapes and shadows, yet contained within an unmistakable sense of dread and woe. It is hard to explain, but it was like an aspect of darkness bled through the seemingly innocent drawings, transforming an otherwise surreal, childlike setting into something deeper, more sinister.

Our parents didn't catch it at first. How could they? Drawings are drawings, right? The amount of random, nonsensical doodles the average kid produces is nothing short of staggering. And who has the time to sift through the ever-growing pile, all the while pretending each and every one is a true masterpiece? No, they did what any parent would do; idly nod and smile, pat Daniel on his head, and assure him it was a beautiful work of art.

Thus they failed to grasp what was really going on. What was actually stirring inside that seemingly pristine mind. Maybe, if they'd just paid more attention, things might have turned out differently? Maybe that dark seed hadn't found room to grow? Wouldn't have sprouted into the madness that followed? I guess we'll never truly know.

Daniel kept this up for weeks before our father finally realised something was brewing. By that time the drawings were taking a more tangible, substantial form; real people, real environments, real horror. They differed slightly in style, like he was experimenting, slowly coming to terms with the story he wanted to tell, but they all had one vital puzzle-piece in common; the pale deformed figure.

It would feature in every drawing he made, wherever it took place. In our living room, kitchen, his bedroom, the bathroom; the figure would always be present in some sense. Harrowing in the background, or staring from a painting on the wall, or barely visible in the obscurity of the crudely drawn shadows. Sometimes it would have a missing limb; a hand, or a foot, but most of the time the limbs were just angled... wrong. Twisted, bent out of shape, distorted, either too long or too short.

The face...

The face was never quite right. Nose in the wrong place. Eyes disturbingly unaligned and disproportioned. Mouth open in the weirdest, most sickening poses. The hair was wild and charcoal black, flowing around the figure in erratic shapes. No wonder then that poor Daniel suddenly faded, his once bright and happy demeanor now replaced by a sullen, gloomy affliction. His once glowing, rosy complexion now ashen-grey and pallid. It was too much for his young shoulders to bear; and it was readily apparent to anyone willing to see it.

And when my parents finally became aware, they hastily dismissed it. Just a phase, or a passing notion, they told him. Even when he pleaded with them, eyes overflowing with tears, they wouldn't listen. The human imagination, they told him, is a powerful thing. Sometimes it may even seem real. Feel real. But it isn't. It's just that; a fantasy, a growing, expanding mind overcome with new and unknown sensations.

"But I've seen it!" he cried, "I've heard it!"

Now, I've never been very close to my parents. We were just way too different, and rarely saw eye to eye on anything. It's just something I have learned to deal with. But they listened to Daniel. Whatever it was, whatever bothered him, they would sit down with him, listen intently as he poured his heart out, and would always end up believing him. That's why it was so devastating to him. For the very first time they just dismissed him out of hand.

"There is no such thing as a Whisper Ghost!" our father yelled. That's what Daniel called the dreadful figure. The Whisper Ghost. It would whisper to him when he slept, and show itself in brief, terrible moments in his dreams. "It's just your imagination! You have to stop with this nonsense!"

They tried to hide it, but I could see it in their faces, clear as day. They were freaking out. Anxious, pained expressions. It even went so far that mother pleaded with me to stop encouraging him. "Please," she'd say, "It won't do anyone any good."

But I had to support my little brother. That's what big sisters do. I was the only one that believed him; that wanted him to resolve and ultimately escape the torment he was in. And I made certain to always assure him that I was there for him.

"Don't worry," I'd murmur softly, "I'll always be here for you. Always have, always will."

It didn't take long before other people started noticing the sudden change in Daniel's behaviour. Teachers, friends, neighbors, relatives; all voicing their heartfelt concern. My parents still wouldn't listen though. "No one decides how we raise our son!"

my father would boom. But they didn't know just how much it affected him. They couldn't have, right? If they did, surely they'd do everything in their power to help him, wouldn't you agree? I mean, that's what parents should do.

I knew we were running out of time. Daniel was a nervous wreck at this point, trembling and sweating, scared out of his mind all day, every day. Soon he'd fade from us all; the flimsy, fragile little mind broken and shattered. I had to wake him up. Make him take action. Convince him to be brave and confront his fears. So I did what little I could.

He would sometimes sneak soundlessly outside my room at night. I guess it gave him comfort to be close to me on some level, and I was happy I could be there for him in those uncertain moments. That night was no different. Only this time I told him what to do. No nonsense-like.

"You have to do it, Daniel," I whispered, "It's your only option. The only way to be free."

He stood there silently for minutes, like he was unable to comprehend what I was saying. I kept repeating it, over and over, until I was sure he understood every last word. It was now or never. If this didn't work, we'd both be in heaps of trouble, and the aftermath would more than likely destroy him.

"Do you understand, Daniel," I whispered, "Do you see now what you have to do?"

He nodded weakly and quietly snuck back to his room. I sat there in the darkness for hours, crossing my fingers, hoping, praying, that everything turned out the way I hoped. It had to. It really, really, really had to. The alternative was just too horrible to even imagine.

I didn't sleep at all that night. Kept my eyes glued to that door. Hardly even blinked. Ears on full alert; every little sound enough to send me into adrenaline-fuelled stupors of anxiety. To be honest, I didn't know what outcome scared me the most. Failure meant pain and heartache. Success meant utter uncertainty; a strange new world. Whatever was coming, my life would forever change, that much remained true.

And when that door opened, I held my breath, bracing myself for the worst, even though I still hadn't come to terms with what exactly that was.

And then came the light. And the screams. And the crying. And the sirens.

Hands, voices, questions, comfort, tears, vomit.

"Holy shit," a man said, tears streaming down his face, "How long have you been down here?"

"Jesus fucking christ," another one chimed in.

"Fucking monsters," a third one murmured from the corner, his fine shirt now stained with puke.

It took my eyes quite some time to get used to the bright light. There were a lot of them in that cramped room. All eyes either fixated on me, or desperately trying to avoid to. Strange men and women, some in uniforms, others in fine suits.

And Daniel.

Sweet, sweet Daniel.

"I knew you could do it," I whispered hoarsely as they carried me away. "I knew you'd save me."

ABOUT THE AUTHOR

Tor-Anders Ulven is a father, husband, and horror fiction writer hailing from the cold mountains of Norway. He became known through his horror alter ego hyperobscure, primarily posting short stories on the vast writing subreddits of NoSleep and ShortScaryStories. He has since had work published in several anthologies, and will continue to expand his dark universe for as long as people dare visit it.

Amazon: https://www.amazon.com/Tor-Anders-Ulven/e/B07Z6QMTSZ
Facebook: https://www.facebook.com/hyperobscure/
Reddit: https://www.reddit.com/r/Obscuratio/
Twitter: https://twitter.com/hyperobscure
Patreon: https://www.patreon.com/hyperobscure
The Cryptic Compendium: https://www.reddit.com/r/TheCrypticCompendium/